2012:
GOLD'S HISTORY SOLVES MANKIND'S MYSTERY

MICHAEL

Reviews

Source Reader (Book 1)

The Two Witnesses and the Religion Cover-Up

"What a fantastic and exceptionally well written book. I feel very confident that my purchase of its sequel as well was a great decision. I can't wait to read it! Thanks for the knowledge Mike."

Sincerely,

Robert Salmon

Ft. Smith, Arkansas

Source Amazon Editorial Reviews (Book 2)

Aliens Gold Tenth Planet

A shocking sequel to the best seller, *The Two Witnesses and the Religion Cover-up*. Read this riveting story of two men as they continue in their pursuit of answers to the mystery of religion. Then they discover shocking evidence all over the Earth of ancient artwork of aliens and flying saucers. Michael suddenly realizes that religions common themes, mimic today's science and our own pursuits of the same. He theorizes, unlike his religious spirit buddy, that the gods/angels are flesh and blood aliens. They came from up and gave us religious symbols that matched today's science. Their reason for creating us is easy to trace, just follow the gold. The space exploration today could only be made possible through the protection and use of gold. It can also repair and make ozone layers. Hence, our mystery and the answer comes full circle. They came from up and we are going up. All made possible with gold. Creating workers/robots and our recreation of ourselves is more evident today than ever. Up, gold, creating and last but not least our addiction to power through beauty of the flesh, lies behind the shocking discoveries of religion's stronghold. Finally Michael ask the world. Could we be the gods/aliens/angels addicted to the outward beauty of mankind? Head molding, reincarnation and prophecy of our inevitable demise supports this reality. But will we want to be saved from ourselves if we are the aliens? I leave you with a famous quote from the Bible that confirms this possibility, "The angels which kept not their first estate but left it for a strange flesh and keep returning like a dog returning to vomit."

Amazon Editorial Review (Book 3)

Read the riveting ending to the previous two books. *The Two Witnesses and the Religion Cover-up* and its sequel *Aliens Gold Tenth Planet*. What a climax to the most exciting trilogy ever in the history of mankind. Could the aliens be the gods/angels of primitive man? These two desperately try to answer the mystery of mankind. Michael is the only one able to finally break free from his religious upbringing/brainwashing and solve the mystery with religions, common theme of up, gold and creation. Read his spell-binding conclusion to the evidence that clearly shows how heaven became a spirit realm but began in space. Heaven is universally up and primitive man has always looked up to the stars of heaven for guidance from their gods. The quote from

Dr. Wendell J. Flanche PhD sums it all up, "The evidence confirms it. Michaels quest to solve mans mystery will astound you. He theorizes that primitive man's ignorance of alien technologies created the magic spirit factor of religion. And ironically it still prevails today, even in the absence of it. This is truly a spectacular scientific discovery!!! Could the most famous man's name confirm his findings that we could be aliens/angels/gods addicted to the outward beauty of mankind? Are we addicted to this power of beauty? I am, Yeshua. Trace mankind's mystery to the pursuit of gold for the gods? Why gold? And why would god need it? What he discovers is shocking because it confirms our past. Gold is crucial for space travel! When we land on another planet they will say we came from up. If we manipulate primates for workers they would say we created them to worship us. If we left them because they became rebellious with their new-found knowledge they would say we were magical and not understand our need for gold. Ultimately it would take thousands of years for them to solve this mystery, but in the meantime they would still have an economy based in gold. This is our history! They

MICHAEL

"MATCH"! What an unbelievable achievement by this author. It appears he has solved the ultimate mystery; mankind, religion, and the universe itself!

2012: Gold's History Solves Mankind's Mystery
By Mike Brumfield

ISBN 0-974039-06-3
Library of Congress Catalog Card Number (Applied For)

Retail $13.75 plus $2.50 shipping.
Expect delivery in two to three weeks.
To order call 931/657-5815.

First Edition, July 2005

Dedication

IF PRIMITIVE man is on another planet, when we land there, he will say we came from up. All ancient religions state this simple scientific fact. We are about to land on a planct for thc first time in our "**SHORT RECORDED HISTORY.**" Could our origins possibly stem from this very scenario, like ancient religion seems to indicate? Could scientifically advanced physical beings have created us?

Our species is still a mystery, and we are going "Up!" How could ancient religious man have done this, when he wasn't global or scientific? It is just one of many coincidences. I propose that religion's **MATCHING** 'scientific" evidence and universal themes could solve our mystery, if we examine it scientifically! If science can do this, will religious people accept the evidence?

Please consider the following "**UNRECORDED**" evidence. I have no agenda, want no followers, and will give all my money to science! My mother is willing to discuss this question about Heaven with me. I want to do it on the Oprah show. Mom is the best. She "finally believes me/the evidence!" Even though she still wants to stay on Earth as a human, in paradise. She doesn't want to be a 'spirit" with God, **MICHAEL**/"Jesus," and the angels.

This is just a result of fear. Fear of the unknown. The Jehovah's Witnesses teach both, and this is so relevant to my theory about us. She is a Jehovah's Witness. I promise you will enjoy our story. It could be anybody's, even yours! So please give it a chance. I beg you for the sake of our children's future. And last, but certainly never the least, I want to dedicate my life and work to the most precious gift in the universe: my loving mother and family. Thank you all so, so much! Without you I am nothing, but with you I am everything.

Paul Villa photo of flying saucer circa 1960.

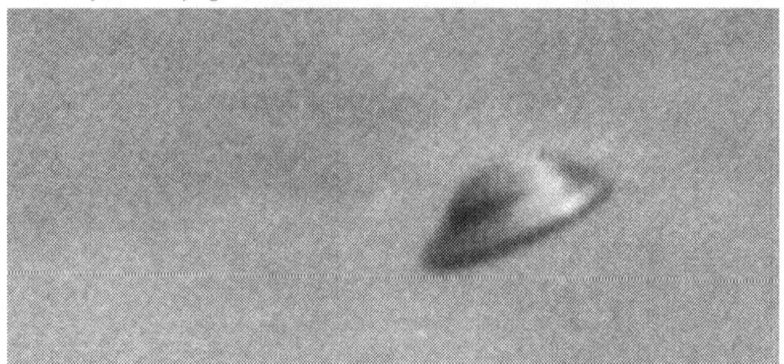

Picture on front cover of book 1980. How can these match when they are taken twenty years apart. Again, these "MATCH" ancient cave drawing on front cover. World's largest saucer on head of Easter Island, and aborigine saucer and alien's gold halo above (page 8) protecting it in space.

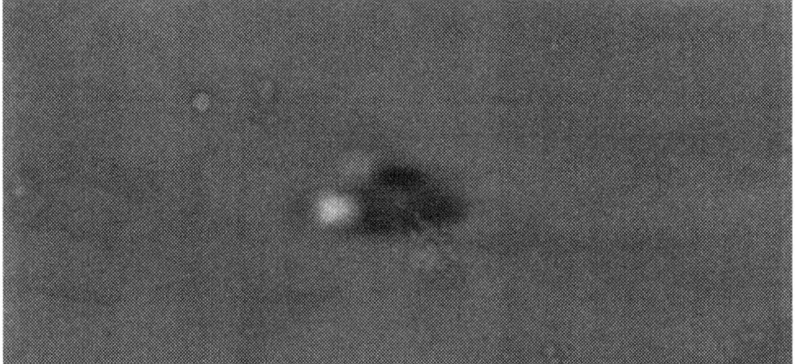

Video taken in 2003 by Jeff Willes of Phoenix, Arizona. To buy video, type his name in computer or call 623/847-9132.

RELIGION IS HISTORY!!!
Missing Link Proof!

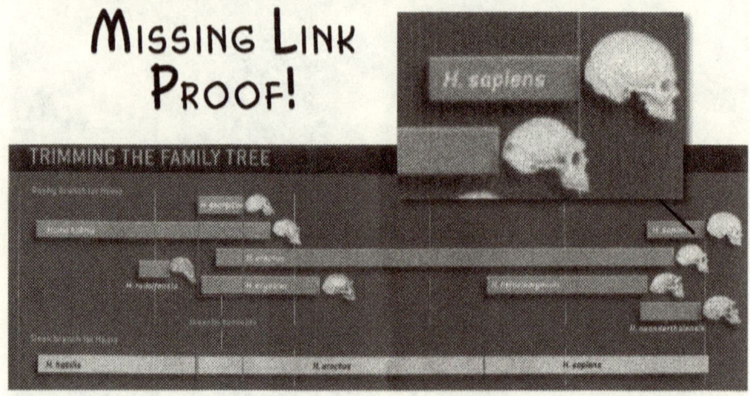

The alien skull shows the obvious mix between primitive man and himself producing us. We are the mystery! See skull on page 5. Religion began approximately 200,000 years ago when our big headed species started burying the dead and making artwork! This coincides with my theory like many others (Erich von Daniken and Alan Alford) that theorize intelligent beings from the sky manipulated primitive man and created this missing link in skull growth. Primitive man remained so for many millions of years without any evolution in knowledge. The only logical explanation for the missing link and inexplicable sudden attainment of knowledge is religion itself. Not slow evolution, but a sudden scientific creation. The fossil evidence supports this reality! Religion is from Heaven or the sky! It is universal in the creation stories; it is clear that we are created to worship them or work for them. We are not linked! It is universal. This work or "purpose" can be traced directly to our first order of business. It was and is gold. It is universal. Gold is important for space travel. We are creating robots to assist in our space travels, which is only made possible with gold! This is universal! Even the robot itself is mostly composed of gold. It is the most resistant protector to the extreme conditions of space. The gold halo is the universal god symbol which is above the head. All gods are depicted as being able to fly. I am presenting the following religious symbols and their matching scientific counterparts as evidence to prove the creation of man was and is a scientific one. I propose that our true purpose is religion's pre-destined will; their pre-determined plan for us. Our true purpose is why they stay away on purpose. Please enjoy the exciting conclusion to my story. See for yourself how science is revealing an unfolding pre-determined plan for mankind that mirrors religion itself. Science today matches religion!

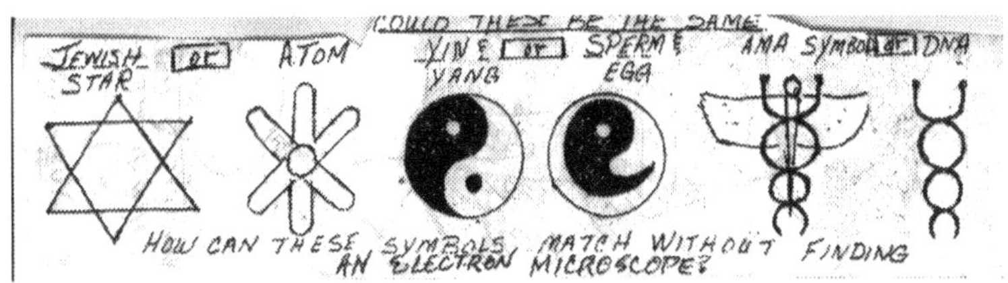

SYMBOLS:

Matching Themes:	Religion	Science
	Omnipresence	Space Program
	Creation/Man	Robots
	Saving Life	Improve/Saving Man's Life
	Multiply	Ensure Propagation of Species
And Others:	Manipulating Age	Genetics for Manipulating Age

Curing of Disease and Ultimately Death

One Mind	Evidence Rules
Levitation	Anti-Gravity
Mummification	Cryogenics
Mental Telepathy	Cybernetics
Spirit	Holograms
Disappearing	Teleportation
Mystery™	Biorhythm Feedback

I'm sure there are many more. So please read on as I "have" to get to work! I'm sure you'll get the point. I propose that religion is not only the best evidence that space is already conquered, but tells us plainly the answer to Fermi's paradox: " Why don't they contact us?"! The world just hasn't come together to scientifically answer it. But of course we all know the world is just now global and capable of destroying itself. These are the two pre-requisites for the end to be ushered in. Coincidence? Our true purpose explains their silence and the reason they stay away on purpose. It is for the good of science. However, this is the end of their tortuous silence. It is the only way to save our planet. It is the next step in their plan. The two witnesses torture the world with their prophecy! Our species is the most unnatural self-destructive species in the universe. Get ready for contact. The "Regeneration of Man", Second Coming, Mayan Golden Age. It is here and happening now!

The Starchild controversy

SINCE FEBRUARY 1999 a bizarre looking skull, known as the Starchild skull, has been exhibited at UFO conferences and heavily discussed in UFO journals.

The Starchild skull is alleged to be the remains of an alien-human hybrid.

Legend of the Star People

According to the Starchild Project, an organization that wants to arrange DNA testing of the skull to prove an incredible origin, the skull was discovered in the mountains of northern Mexico. Indian tribes from the region have legends of Star People – beings from the sky who visit Earth to impregnate local women before returning years later to retrieve the hybrid infants.

A hybrid is a cross between two different breeds or species. Only closely related species can interbreed or "hybridize," and it seems unlikely that humans and aliens would be similar enough.

Big head

The skull has several strange features that suggest it is not human. It has a massive brain capacity, flattened rear, shallow eye sockets, and is missing the front sinuses.

The Starchild Project claims to have consulted over 50 experts, the vast majority of whom argue that the skull is that of a deformed human child.

Most experts say that the Starchild skull is that of a child suffering from hydrocephaly, a disease in which fluid builds up on the brain and makes the skull swell.

■ The Starchild skull *is far from normal. But is it from an abnormal or cradle-boarded human infant, or perhaps an alien-human hybrid?*

It is also widely thought that the skull has been cradle-boarded. Cradle-boarding is the practice of strapping an infant's head to a board and causes flattening of the back of the skull. It was practiced in the area of Mexico where the skull comes from. The Starchild Project argues that close examination of the skull rules out this explanation, and is attempting to raise funds to pay for DNA testing – the only way to be certain of the skull's origins.

"Beings from the sky" Is this the Owl Man, page 6, which looks like an alien? He is pointing up! The skull supports this reality. Also "impregnates women" supports the cover art of the mother goddess statue, yet also has a big head! Skull is evidence of aliens being flesh and blood and these "sons of God" in Genesis 6:4. It supports my theory that they are not religious "spirit" magical beings. However, I conclude the atom, which makes everything, is "religion's invisible spirit" creator, evolving scientifically through time, not by magic. Read on. It scientifically fits religion's invisible omnipresent God.

DNA similarities make world seem smaller

Survey says any two people 99.9 percent identical

By LEE BOWMAN
Scripps Howard News Service

Although everyone's genetic makeup is unique, scientists have found that populations from different parts of the world still share more genetic similarities than had been thought.

The results of a computer analysis of DNA from individuals representing 52 populations around the globe, published today in the journal Science, make up the largest such global survey of genetic diversity, and should help studies of ancient human migrations.

Those surveyed were broken into five regions: Africa, Eurasia, East Asia, Oceania and the Americas. Differences among individuals within those groups accounted for 93%-95% of genetic variety, according to the international team led by Marcus Feldman, a professor of humanities and sciences at Stanford University.

Compare the genetics of any two people, and the matchup will be about 99.9% identical. The research team accurately pinpointed the ancestral content of virtually every individual from Africa, East Asia, Oceania and the Americas. ■

---

1. How could Hopi medicine man know of five races, let alone the alien god? See illustration page 6.

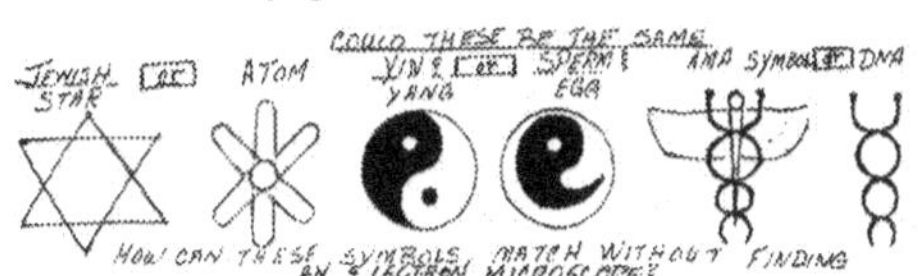

Alien statues found along banks of Jordan River 10,000 years old

2. Notice alien head on mother goddess statue. This supports what gods look like in Genesis 6:4. Statue dated circa 5000 years old found in Jerusalem, Israel.

3. Notice asexual organs on alien statue. This confirms Yeshua's description of angels and explains why they don't give their hand in marriage. They must be androgynous.

Mother goddess statues represent the inevitable separation that was to occur. According to religion mankind is predestined. It happened because the "sons of gods" thought the daughters of men were pretty. Their "giant" offspring became men of great renown and all wickedness spread all over the earth. This exemplifies their lust for power due to their obvious oneness in looks and small size. And they must have considered themselves ugly. It took place during the mysterious time frame, of the last ice age approximately 13,000 years ago up to the beginning of the Jewish calendar, 4000 BC (6,000 years ago). These are found all over the earth. The alien headed one is from Israel circa 8000 years old. The round headed one is 30,000 years. It is called the Venus of Willendorf. The asexual alien statue was found along the banks of the Jordan River. Notice the circles as if they knew about chromosomes and DNA. These as all scientists agree were religiously important and found in every household. I theorize that like the pyramids and Easter Island giants they were left to stand the test of time to tell us what their gods look like and where they are, Aliens and space.

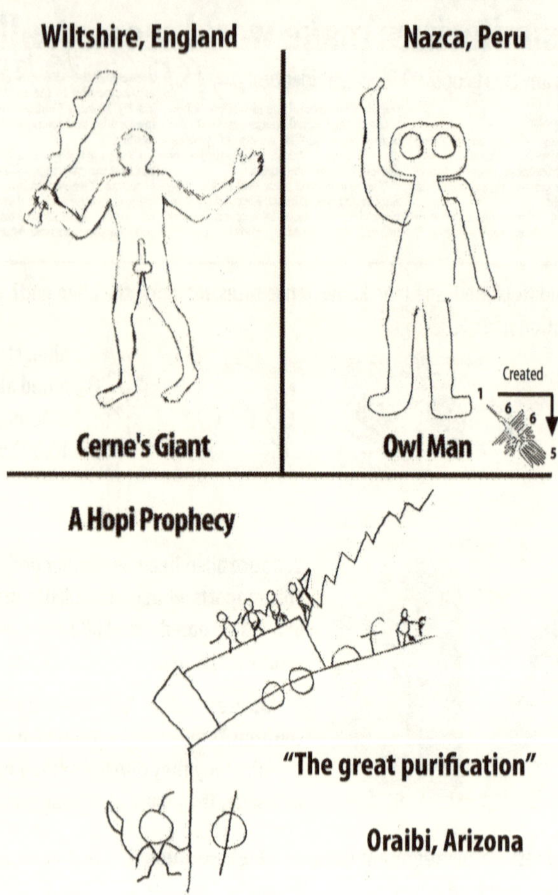

The Cerne's Giant tells us why they couldn't cohabit with their creation of modern man (we kill for sex) and when they will return. (Three humps on club indicate an impending nuclear disaster. Atom has three parts.) The Owl Man tells us where their gods live and what they look like, space and aliens. It has a hummingbird which represents fertility pointing at it. Count the appendages and see connection to biblical number of man 666 and five races. The Hopi prophecy again shows us an alien god (big headed guy) saving the earth from destruction and recycling the majority of man up, obviously to another planet. Again how did the shaman know of the five races of man let alone an alien God? Notice similarity of box carrier to today's truck trailer. Feather on head indicates gods' ability to fly. See saucer attached to his arm.

The Five Faces of Man

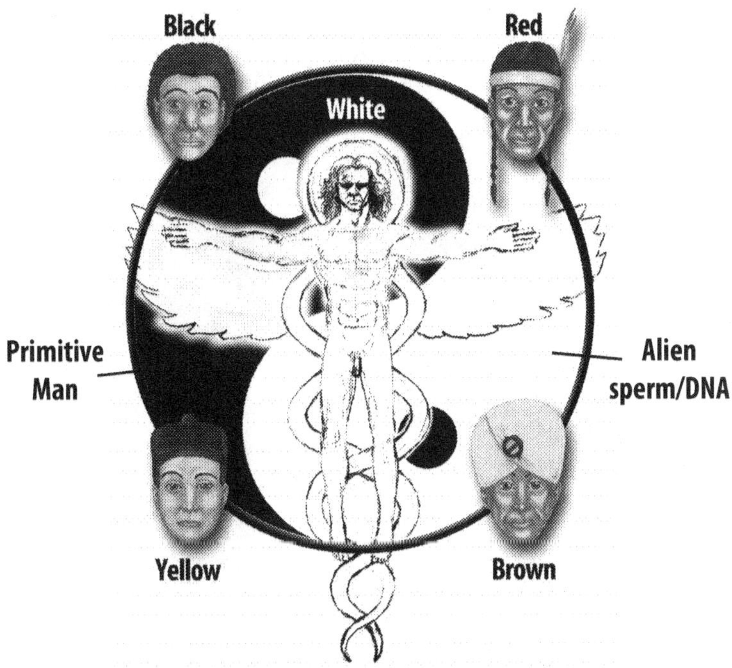

The different colors and facial structures indicate the competition to make the "prettiest" human. This "prettiest" factor is evident in Genesis 6:4 and the fall of the angel story!

Looks give us power over one another. All religions have a fall from heaven and earth being one, void and without form, to being separated. The gods/angels live in space—Earth's become prison. This resulted from a power struggle. The biblical account gives us two creations. Nature created primitive man and then the gods/angels/aliens scientifically created modern man as a worker. Modern man is the mystery. The evidence universally points to mining gold. This started 100,000 years ago and continues to this day! The matching yin and yang and AMA symbol to the science symbols of the sperm/egg and DNA reflects our scientific creation. Even the biblical account describes a scientific process both for the man and the woman. The woman's creation is from man and he is anesthetized. Ultimately, I theorize two ongoing infinite creations: Nature's gods/angels/white sperm/DNA and us from primitive man/black sperm/DNA. We are the mystery!

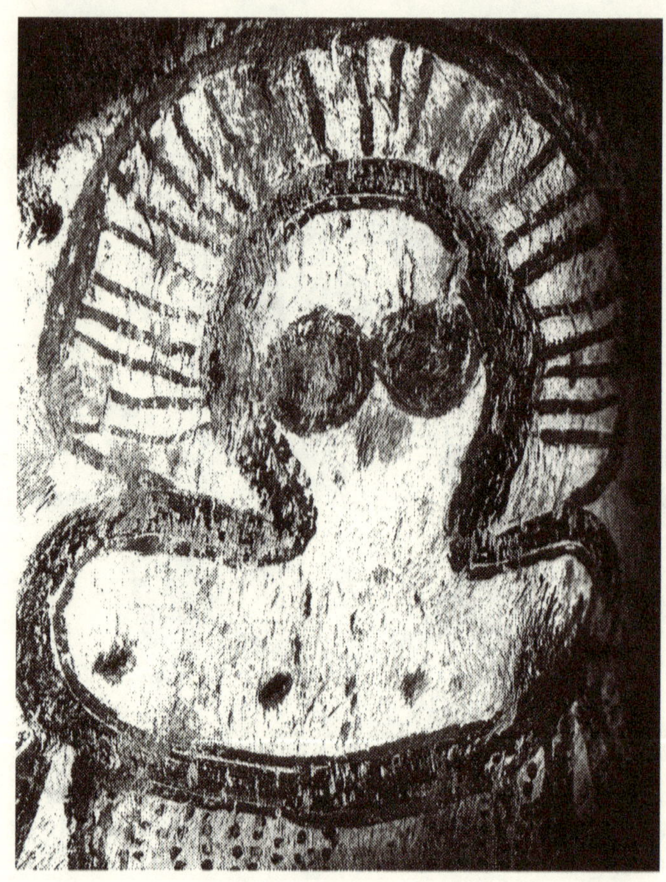

This is the most important evidence because it shows us, what their gods looked like (aliens), what they came and live in (flying saucers) and why they needed gold (space life and exploration). Hence we have the Biblical quote "Heaven's streets are paved with gold." It is a universal religious theme. Heaven is space, up to primitive man.

Cave drawing of aboriginal god Wandjina. Notice similarity to Owl Man. Also see halo around above head. This supports 10th planet story of gold replacing ozone and "who" was mining it before they created man as a "tiller of the ground" in Genesis. Man's purpose supports skeletal discoveries in gold mines. Gold protects astronauts from dangerous life radiation in space.

MOST IMPORTANTLY This solves pyramid mystery. Gold is found most in quartz which forms natural pyramid shape.

These gold artifacts are from Erich Von Daniken's book *Gold of the Gods*.

Gold artifact from ancient mine in Peru. Notice two alien-looking beings holding snakes and third one at top inside pyramid. The circles look like stem cells, atoms or eggs that are fertilized.

This connects pyramids to aliens. The pyramid served as image of rock that contained gold, quartz.

Alien-looking figure, right, has pyramid on head, penis and snake/DNA halo. The Bible says (Luke 6:4) "Only the Father in Heaven is God." Erich theorizes the skeleton on left could be a coded disk for message to contact future man. It is made of aluminum and coated in gold. We sent a coded disk into space with the same composition. I, again, see DNA, cells/eggs and chromosomes. The skeleton's head has a **HALO** around it. See horned face like Africa rock art and Israel statures. The skeleton represents our deadly creation. We kill and according to Yeshua, we are the dead. "He is the firstborn from the dead." Do we all have to take a turn being him?

Gold is the most ancient metal known to man and sacred to religion, everywhere. This information is provided by World's Leading Gold Mining Co.

History of Gold - Timeline

4000 BC	Gold is first known to be used in parts of Central and Eastern Europe.
3000 BC	The Egyptians master the arts of beating gold into leaf and alloying gold with other metals t variations in hardness and color. They also develop the ability to cast gold, using the lost-wa still used in today's jewelry industry. The Sumer civilization of southern Iraq uses gold to create a wide range of jewelry, often us sophisticated and varied styles still worn today.
2500 BC	Gold jewelry is buried in the Tomb of Djer, the king of the first Egyptian dynasty, at Abydos,
1500 BC	The immense, gold-bearing regions of Nubia make Egypt a wealthy nation, as gold become recognized standard medium of exchange for international trade. The Shekel, a coin originally weighing 11.3 grams of gold, is used as a standard unit of mea throughout the Middle East. The coin contained a naturally occurring alloy called electrum, v approximately two-thirds gold and one-third silver.
1352 BC	The young Egyptian King Tutankhamen is interred in a pyramid tomb laden with gold, his re an extravagant gold anthropoid sarcophagus.
1350 BC	The Babylonians begin to use fire assay to test the purity of gold.
1091 BC	Squares of gold are legalized in China as a form of money.
560 BC	The first coins made purely from gold are minted in Lydia, a kingdom of Asia Minor.
58 BC	Julius Caesar seizes enough gold in Gaul (France) to repay Rome's debts.
50 BC	The Romans issue a gold coin called the Aureus.
600-699 AD	The Byzantine Empire resumes gold mining in central Europe and France, an area undevel fall of the Roman Empire. Artisans of the period produce intricate gold artifacts and icons.
1100	1100 Venice secures its position as the world's leading gold bullion market due to its locatio trade routes to the east.
1284	Venice introduces the gold Ducat, which soon becomes the most popular coin in the world, so for more than five centuries. Great Britain issues its first major gold coin, the Florin, which is followed by the Noble, the A Crown, and the Guinea.
1511	King Ferdinand of Spain sends explorers to the Western Hemisphere with the command to '
1717	Isaac Newton, Master of the London Mint, sets price of gold that lasts for 200 years.
1787	First US gold coin is struck by Ephraim Brasher, a goldsmith.
1792	The Coinage Act places the young United Sates on a bimetallic silver/gold standard, definin Dollar as equivalent to 24.75 grains of fine gold, and 371.25 grains of fine silver.
1803	North Carolina site of first US gold rush. The state supplies all the domestic gold coined for the US Mint in Philadelphia until 1828.
1848	The California gold rush begins when James Marshall finds specks of gold in the water at Jo sawmill near the junction of the American and Sacramento Rivers.
1850	Edward Hammond Hargraves, returning from California, predicts he will find gold in Australi week. He discovers gold in New South Wales within one week of landing.
1859	The Comstock Lode of gold and silver is discovered in Nevada. As a result, Nevada is made years later.

Oldest gold mines found in Africa civilization traced from NE Africa science traces our origin to hominid they named "Eve."

Genesis Project

Capsule bearing solar secrets

By PAUL FOY
Associated Press

SALT LAKE CITY — In a harrowing feat high over the Utah desert Wednesday, two helicopter stunt pilots will try to snatch a floating space capsule that holds "a piece of the sun" and bring it safely down.

Their biggest fear: What if they flub it on live TV?

And that's entirely possible. The pilots rate it 8 or 9 on a difficulty scale of 10.

"It's like flying in formation with a giant floating jellyfish," says pilot Dan Rudert.

The stuntmen will be trying to hook the 400-pound Genesis capsule as it hurtles 400 feet a minute. Inside it are fragile solar wind particles — so small they're invisible — which scientists hope will reveal clues about the origin of our solar system.

The biggest challenge, pilots say, will be flying at 40 mph almost a mile above the desert without visual reference points to judge distance or speed as they close in with hook and cable.

The helicopter pilots will have five chances to snag the capsule in midair. Military pilots were unavailable for a mission that required them to commit to a task six years in the future. The civilian pilots have replicated the retrieval without fumbles in dozens of practice runs, but are terrified of failing as NASA television broadcasts a worldwide feed.

If they miss and the Genesis capsule hits the ground hard, scientists say they'd have to spend months sorting through broken jewelry-studded disks holding the tiny solar wind particles.

There are other opportunities for the $260 million mission to go awry, too. For NASA engineers a white-knuckle moment will be when the capsule must be steered through a "keyhole" high in the Earth's atmosphere. If the experts at California's Jet Propulsion Laboratory can't line up the precise entry and angle, Genesis will be waved off on an elliptical orbit of Earth, and another attempt would be made in six months.

The Genesis mission marks the first time NASA has collected and returned any objects from farther than the moon, said Roy Haggard, Genesis' flight operations chief and CEO of Vertigo Inc., which designed the capture system.

Together, the charged atoms captured on the capsule's disks of gold, sapphire, diamond and silicone are no bigger than a few grains of salt, but scientists say that's enough to reconstruct the chemical origin of the sun and its family of planets.

Scientists will keep busy for five years after Genesis completes its ride to Earth.

This clearly shows our need for gold in space as well as other "precious" metals and gems. This explains religion's description of the same in heaven/space. After all, religion is universally anti-wealth.

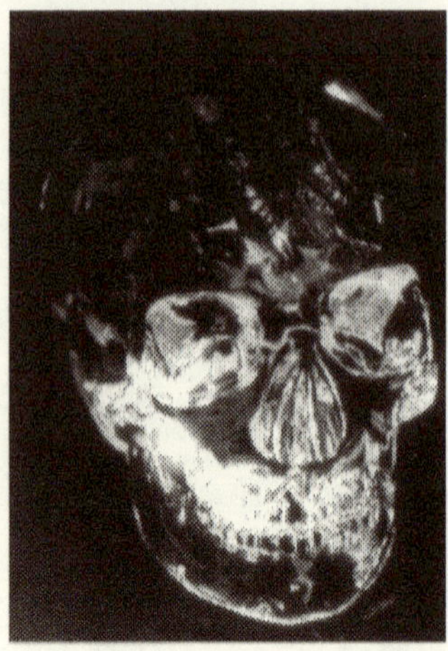

One of thirteen Mayan quartz crystal skulls. They are anatomically perfect, ancient and show no tool marks. Legend has it that they hold information that will solve our mystery which is where are the people/gods who made us and them?

This is where I propose they are. This is a statue from Easter Island that is looking up and appears to have a flying saucer on top of his head to tell us why they are in these religious fiery chariots of the sky.

Famous NASA Tether Incident

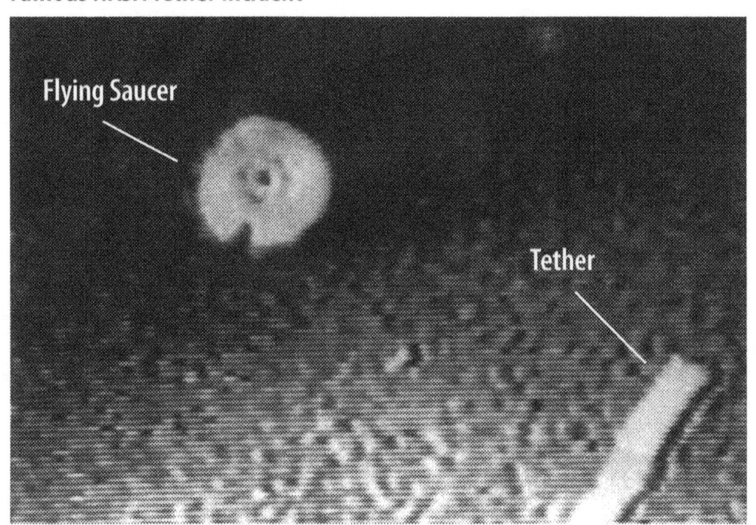

Saucer looks like galaxy, yin and yang, and the atom.

Galaxy has black hole in center which emits white hole.

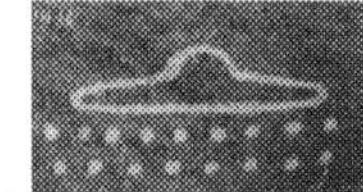

Sombrero Galaxy

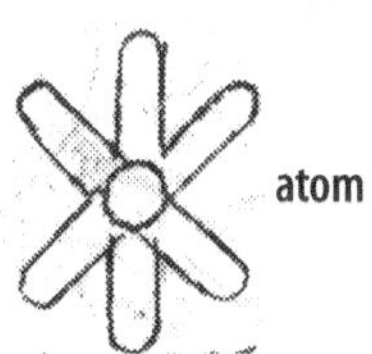

Could spinning be key to anti-gravity? Is Event Horizon proof time can be stopped? Can all life be related to atomic structure? Does knowledge of atom answer life's mystery?

Religious ancient disk and obelisk on left from China. See three dots at top of obelisk. Does this represent atomic propulsion? Ancient clay disk on right from Turkey.

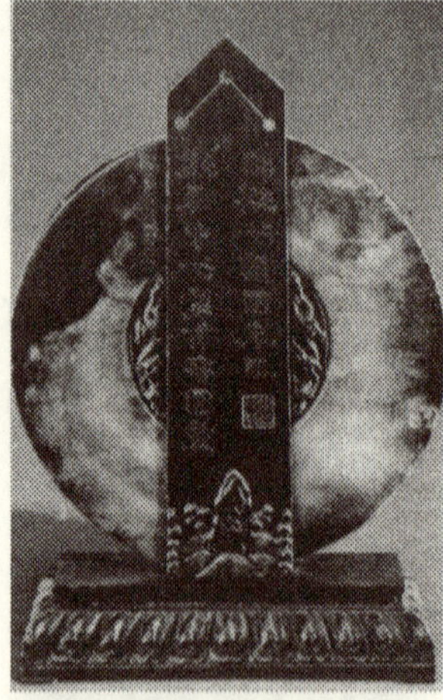

Ancient gold disk from Bogota, Columbia, matches clay mold from Turkey and flying saucers' shape.

See notches on outside perimeter! Important because it matches many others from other countries. All ancient.

Gold disk from Peru gold mine. See sperm and alien head and face. The center is full of atoms. There are faces in sun and stars. We are stardust/atoms/adams. Notice diamond infinity symbol.

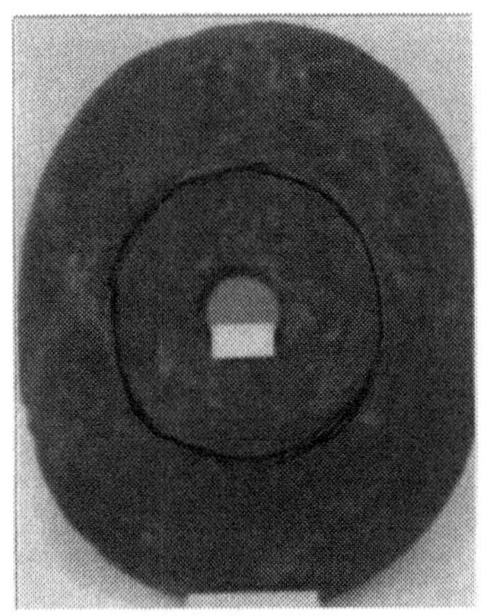

Ancient Yap stones "money stones" from the South Pacific. These are still used for money today, although it is rare. They look like the NASA tether saucer and all other ancient disks.

This ancient disk was found in Ohio, my home state. It is a beautiful piece of evidence to support my theory. It has an eye in the middle of the "right" hand which is center of disk. This clearly represents the gods being in control, knowing all (omniscience) and controlling all (omnipotent). The rattlesnakes represent our deadly creation. The disks give them omnipresence.

Ancient cave art from Ubekestan. See notches like in Ohio and spirals like dropa stones. Besides, he looks like an astronaut. See atom symbol on jaw line.

Ancient Chinese gold disk with rubies. It says "anywhere the sun shines, life will exist." This looks like a computer chip. The disk fits disk on Genesis probe.

Looks just like other UFOs of NASA!

These are dropa stones from Tibet and are circa 10000 years old. They were found deep in a cave with the remains of about 400 skeletons of little people with big heads. The island of Yap values an identical stone as money. They are called money stones. The largest ones measure up to 10 feet, and are made of polished white limestone. The whiter they are the more valuable. Now we see where the white thing comes from in religion. If these gods stay in spaceships they would be really white looking. The universal alien is the Roswell gray! If you don't buy this then buy an alien doll. It will be him!

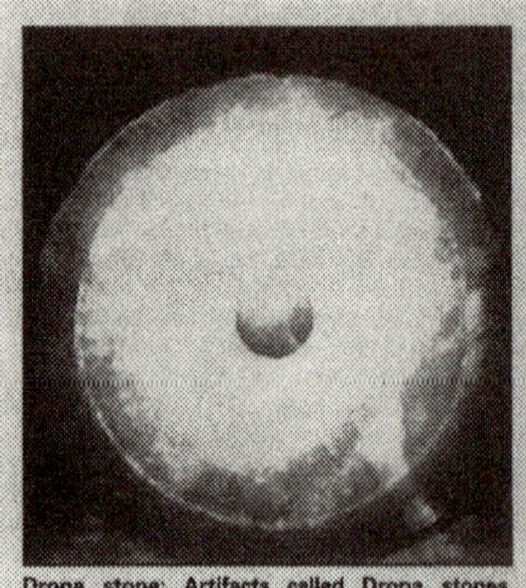

Dropa stone: Artifacts called Dropa stones, which bear an uncanny resemblance to the UFOs involved in the tether incident.

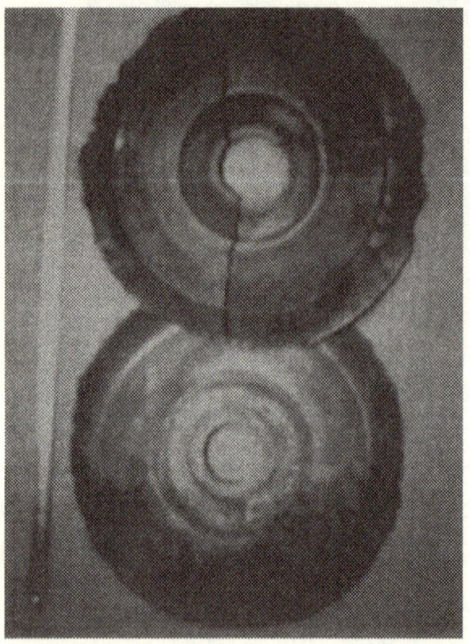

Last but not least, the Legend tells how they were attacked and eventually killed off by neighboring tribes because they were so "UGLY." Here again is evidence why they can't co-habit with us and how language comes full circle to support the evidence and answer the big question, "Where did they come from; What do they look like and why do they stay away?" They "dropped" out of sky according to legend and this is why the tribes they spawned are called Dropas. They still exist today and have physical attributes that resemble the alien. The Owl Man is your next answer and Cernes Giant the cast of the three WWWs. Where, what, why!

"Ancient" bronze disk from Norway. Gold overlay of sun, moon and objects in sky. The holes on outer perimeter look just like ones on disk from Turkey, Ohio and notches from Dropa stones. Notice seven circles like atoms between sun and moon!

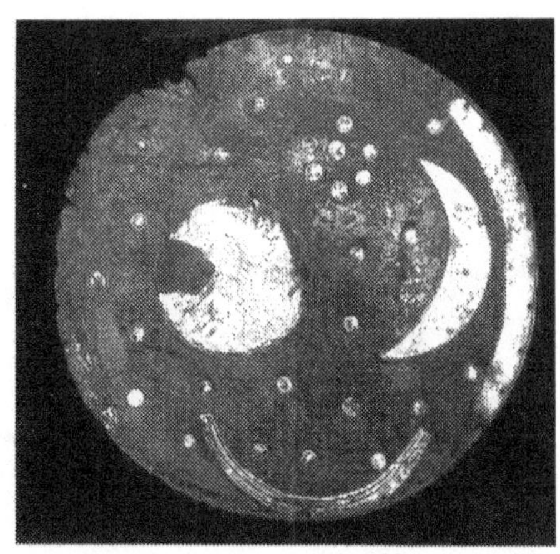

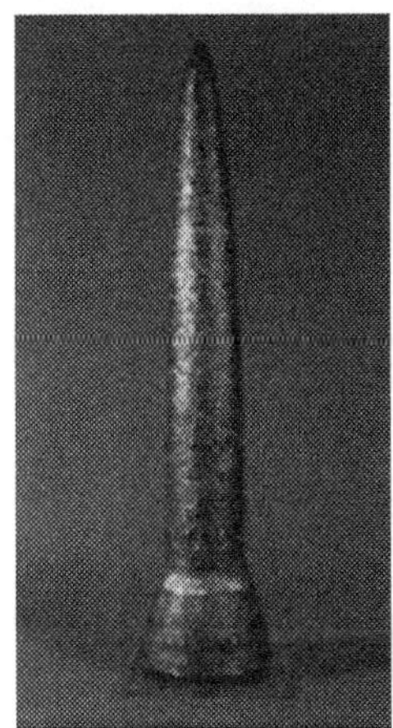

Mysterious ancient gold cone hats of Europe. They look like rockets and have flying saucers images as well as moons and suns. The priests wore these as hats.

This ancient Egyptian sculpture of Ahknenton has a religious ceremonial hat that resembles the gold cone and Easter Island.

Again, these disks, hats, gold, and obelisks all implicate and match flying saucer evidence and explain why they depict stars in space. It is already conquered by space faring beings that created our mysterious species to mine gold. Gold is crucial to explore space!

Ancient Egyptian relief "Stellae" of Ahknenton, Nefertiti, and children. Notice bald elongated heads and big alien eyes!

Egyptian papyrus clearly show Ahknenton's head without hat. It is alien looking like long limbs and fingers. The bald head is universal religious practice like ancient head molding!

These were found in
Iraq. They are ancient
statues of gods. The
one on the right shows
cloning.

These clearly prove
androgynous beings.
Squiggly lines are DNA.

These look like head of mother goddess statue.

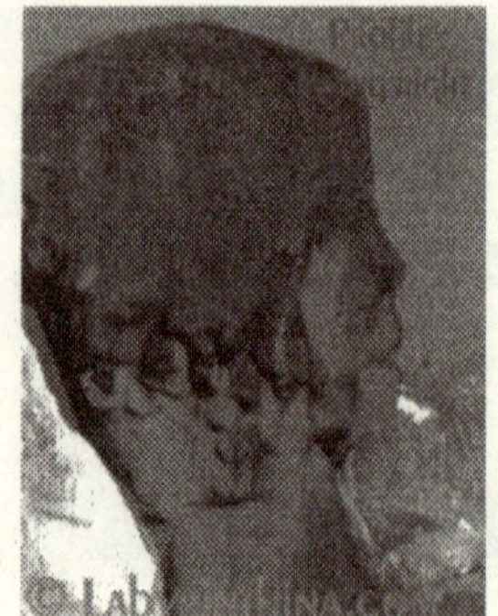

Ancient sculpture shows alien head and man's head together!

Ancient religious sculptures that match from three different continents!

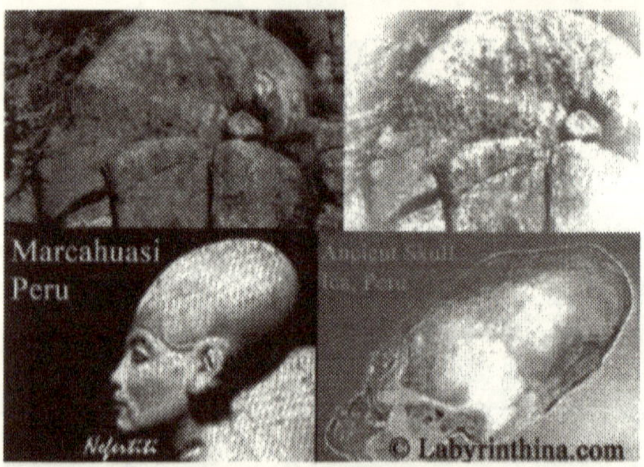

More matches! Ica, Peru has Ica stones that tell and show my theory. Alien-looking gods here with primitive man and dinosaurs creating our species, the mystery/modern man.

Ancient stone carvings from Peru.

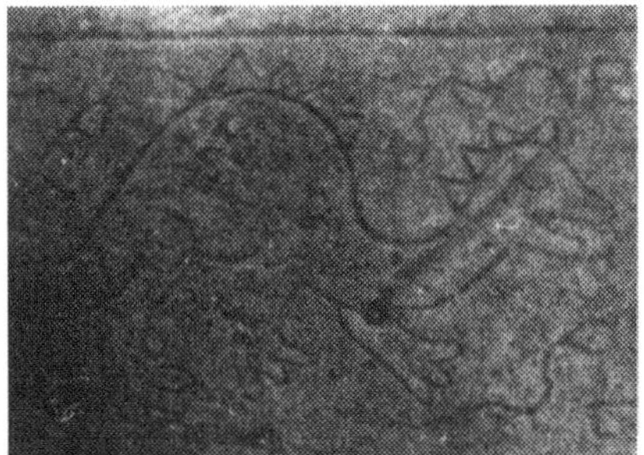

Notice sperm-like objects with **DINOSAUR!** Also amulet on right clearly shows big headed alien god above earth and not on it. He's holding "7" pointed sun and "half" moon. The earth is gridded like we do today with latitude and longitude lines. How is any of this possible without space already being conquered by scientific beings?

Giant stones of Costa Rica.

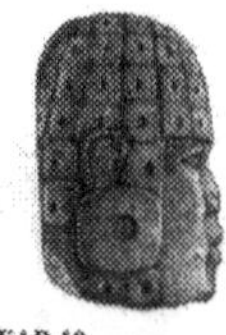

These are six-foot giant heads of the Olmecs. Giant Heads! Notice DNA symbol and cross symbol of tenth planet on jaguar head at left. This mirrors sphinx. The right head has "six" claws on forehead and symbol of atom, cell or fertilized egg!

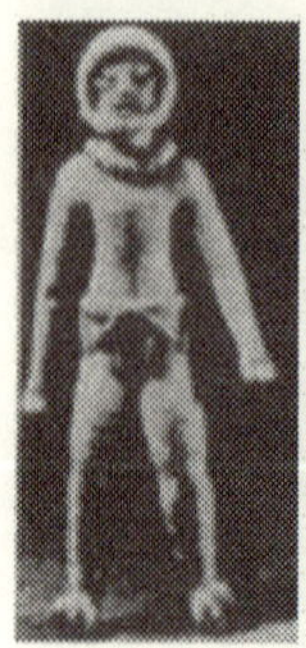

Maya god has gold halo above his obvious spacesuit. This makes it clear, gold is used to protect us in space! This evidence speaks for itself. These are ancient astronaut statues compared to a real one. The bottom one is identical. It was found in Peru and is 6,000 years old.

Also, these are airplane statues made of solid gold. This support space travel's need for gold and proves gods are flesh and blood beings who have already conquered space!

THESE SPEAK FOR THEMSELVES AS WELL. They are all made of gold. From Egypt to Peru!

India

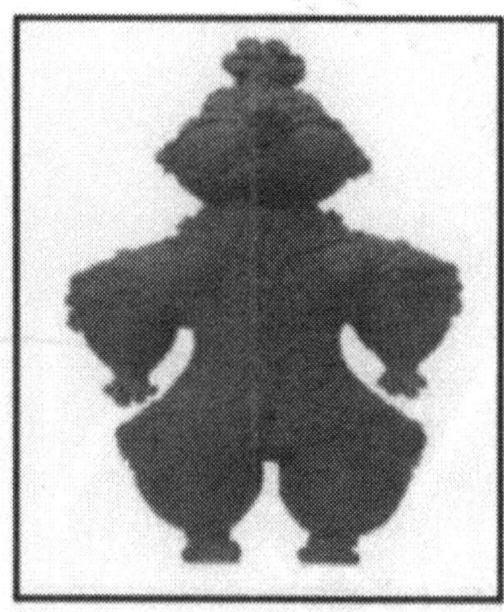

Look at alien eyes!

Turkey

Look at matching thrusters on obvious rocket. The head is missing on pilot.

More ancient statues

Ancient European astronauts!

Mexico Gold Star God
Alien head on DNA from sun bottom left hand.

Brazil
Kayapo tribe still celebrates the legend of "Teacher from Heaven" Bep Kororot; this is his suit; stick, his "fire" stick. He made the villagers' weapons turn to dust when they tried to "attack" him. He helped them and then went to mountain top and disappeared in a cloud of thunder. They await his "**Return**"!

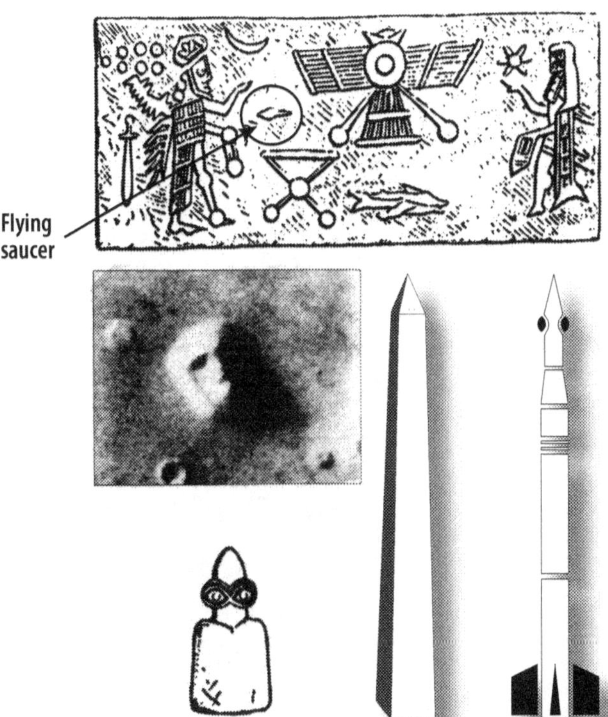

1. Notice the satellite on the clay tablet going from Earth (7th planet) to Mars (6th planet). It looks just like ones today. This tablet is also circa 13000 years. Also notice symbol for Mars matches atom and Jewish star. Is this proof that Mars could have had Man there first and we destroyed it with nuclear weapons? The "man" on mars is in a suit. Is it reason for contact?

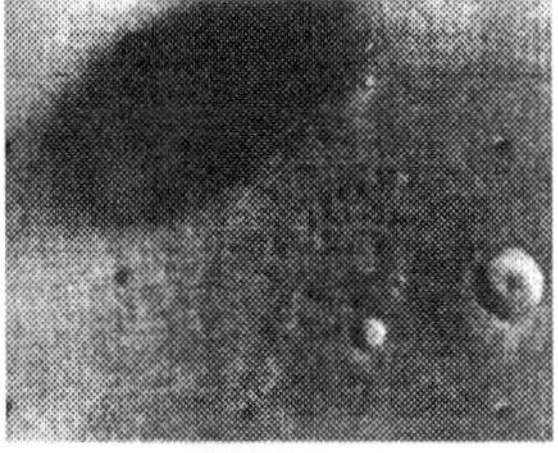

2. See how the helmet of Mars "man" matches our pictures of face on Mars.

3. Notice ancient satellite looks like alien head and eyes of nuclear missile. Egyptian obelisk matches nuclear missile. Egyptians called obelisks shem "rocketship".

4. See flying saucer monitoring earth on mars clay tablet.

5. This is a photo from phobos satellite sent to view mars moon phobos. It is irregular shaped and appears to be hollow. Could it be used as a space base on the inside? We think asteroids could be used this way as natural spaceships. This is the last picture it took before it was deemed "destroyed" by space debris. Looks like a flying saucer to me.

There are many legends of gods from the sky, in clouds that make thunder. The Kayopo story on the previous page mirrors that of Moses and his "ten commandments." They were also to teach us. Could this be the cloud of thunder? Actual photo taken by Army private in 1965. Eyewitnessed by others and never explained!

The bronze statue is from Kiev and is circa 8000 years old. It has six fingers supporting the existence and authenticity of the Roswell Alien autopsy. The recovered dead alien had six fingers and toes. This figure also supports the need for gold as protection in space. It has a Halo. Compare it to the following aboriginal gods. They look alien and even have gold painted halos around their heads. The Aztec block shows two hands intertwined with six fingers. These hands alone represent their god's creation of them and the entanglement represents DNA, how they were created. These match our medical symbol, intertwined serpents. How can they match when it takes an electron microscope to see them? The gods must be scientifically advanced!

Giants of Easter Island South Pacific

Notice the saucer on top of head tells us where they live just like owl man, aboriginal god, and Starchild legend spaceships just like front covers. Six strands of rock looks like DNA readouts. It also could implicate the sixth chromosome mystery or the Jewish creation on the sixth day. Giants were the offspring of gods and "pretty" daughters of man. This is when our separation occurred because wickedness spread all over the earth. A great flood followed. This is a red figure that symbolized mankind. See how he is doing the mystery or transcendental meditation.

The six strands of rock below the Alien looking god could symbolize a DNA readout. I am intrigued by it being six strands. The day of man's biblical creation is the 6th. The Hopi prophecy has six beings (five of man, one of an alien). The hummingbird of the owl man in Nazca reflects this theme as does the biblical "devil". Is it possible that the sixth chromosome is the source of this "looks' manipulation. I've been reading a fascinating book called "The Sixth Chromosome". There are many other things pointing to creation involving the number six like the atom and Jewish star's number of points. The planet mars is the sixth from the tenth. There's more read on! Also, look at man meditating/doing mystery. He is made of red lava rock and is similar to many other representations of first religious worship. Red also represents blood and creation. Mystery worship is universal from Buddhism to sitting Indian style. (See statue of Indian from Tennessee at end of book) Also notice black moai that looks somewhat different from the whiter standing ones. This parallels black and white yin and yang. It also parallels Mayan statues on next page.

This is religion's game of Olmecs from Mexico. They are also known for mysterious carvings of huge heads!

 Figure circled is made of red lava rock like Easter Island man doing mystery. This is what power struggle of gods is about, us. Red symbolizes creation. Notice opposing sides black and white like Easter Island Man and Yin and Yang. Notice six obelisks like stones. Coincidence? Don't think so. Notice similarities to Easter Island statues, Israel statues, aborigines, all other "big headed" God statues from every continent.

The figures are all black and white "facing" each other. The one in the back that is porous looking is the only red one. Could this represent the power struggle over mankind's inevitable creation and does it involve the sixth chromosome? Also, notice the clear resemblance to the alien statue from Israel and the head on the mother goddess statue as well. It clearly looks like the Easter Island heads except for the elongation. They are the product of the mix between the sons of gods/aliens and man. I think losing the bulbous head was the first indicator of their pursuit toward outward beauty. The story supports this with their reason for mixing in the first place. (See back cover)

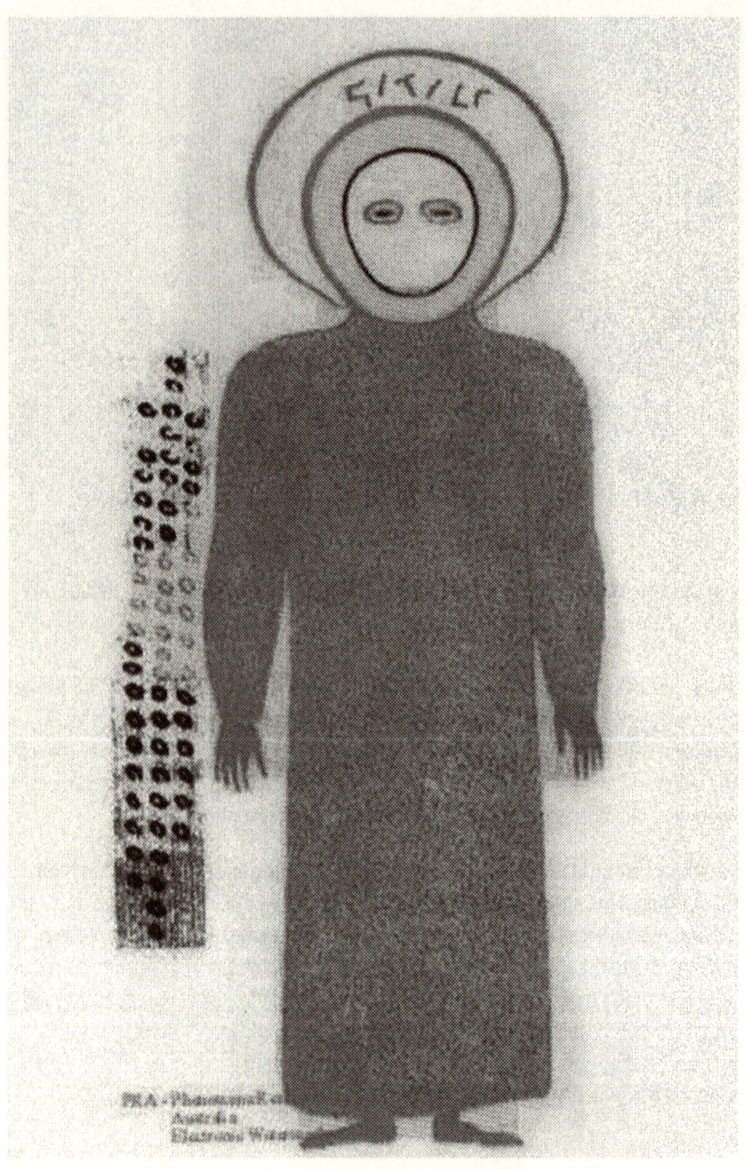

Aborigine cave drawing dated circa 30000 years old. Notice hieroglyphics on gold halo. See more on following page. Also notice readout similar to Easter Island one .These rock layouts/DNA readouts are common across the earth.

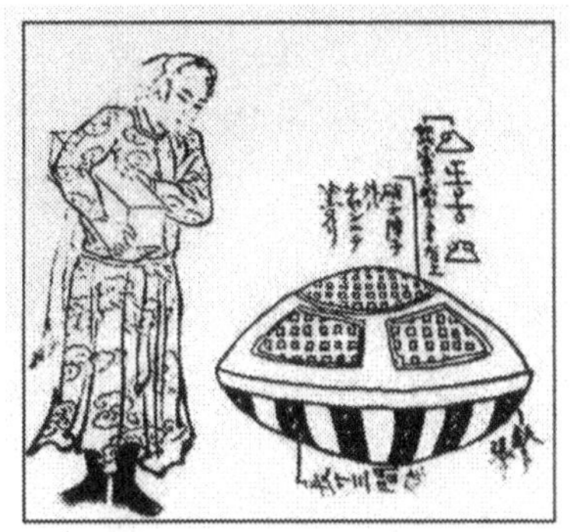

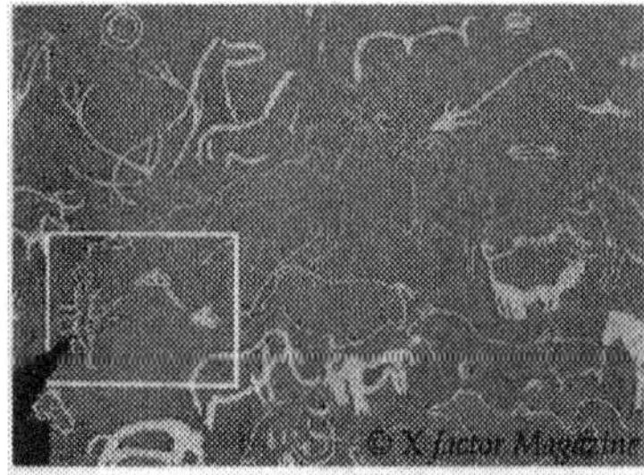

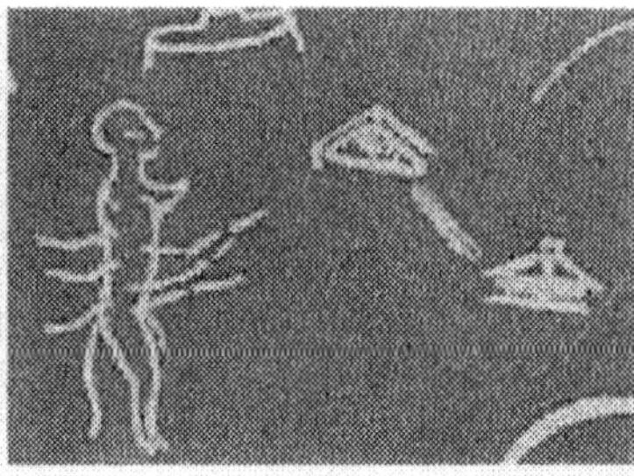

Japanese discovery on the island now known as Taiwan. It is a drawing by a general that discovered a strange ship on the island. This happened in 1806! Notice the ships drawn above it. He found this drawing on the hull of the ship. The writing looks like the hieroglyphics found on the aboriginal gods halo and supports the description of Roswell's.

The cave art clearly shows matching saucers. This is dated circa 15000 years old. It is in France. It shows smaller ships coming out of a large one and abduction! The lines represent the invisible energy taking the human up. The top right picture is the oldest rock of aliens from Africa date circa 50000 years old. It shows the little alien/Roswell gray in control observing. He's even protected by a box that looks much like a tree trimmer's carriage. The others are larger and restraining one of their own. They must have first made themselves larger to be more able to control their scientific manipulations of primitive man. They are obviously serving the little guy and they are struggling with one of their own. Anyway, this supports the scientific manipulation of themselves. See the one with the horns. Is this what gave us the first images of the biblical "devil". Read on! See similarity to statues on following page.

These reptilian looking skulls are found in Ubaid, Iraq. They look like the reptilian looking tall ones on the rock art of the previous page. Scientists have repeatedly mistaken
the eyes for sunglasses or goggles. However they are very similar to the large slanted
eyes of the Roswell gray alien. They are identical to the eyes of the mother goddess
statue from Israel. Notice one is a divided looking skull, giving it the appearance of
hornlike appendages, while the other is elongated. They are clearly two different types.
Were these a product of the first attempts to make themselves larger for power or for
mining gold. Anyway, it is clear here and in the writings that scientific creation was
producing things like this, the mothman, centaur and other abnormalities. The little
guy with a HUGE head is from Utah! See appendages (Devil's horns?).

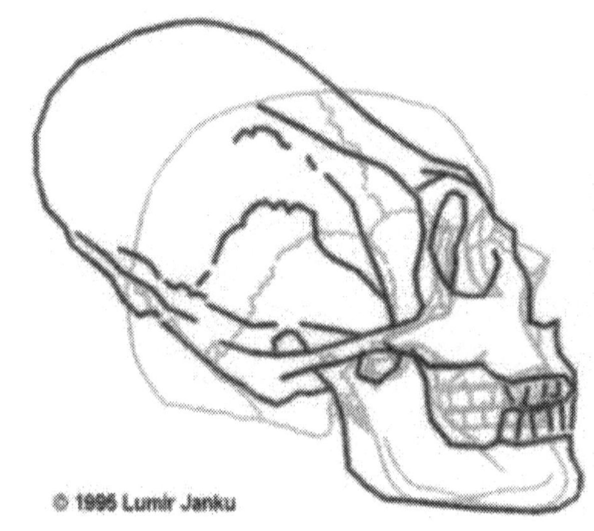

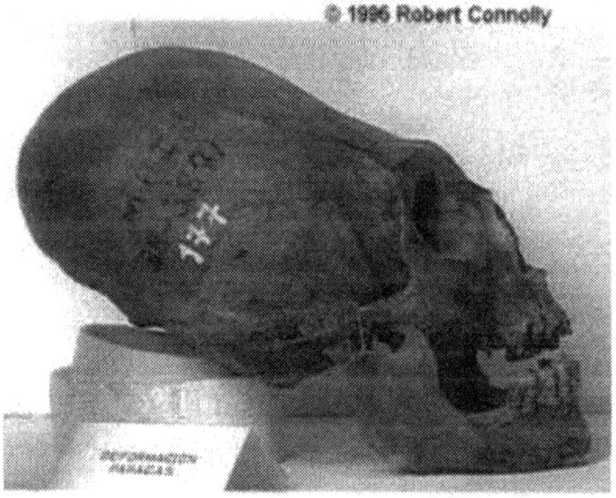

Head molding was an ancient universal religious practice! Obviously, they were trying to imitate their gods' appearance.

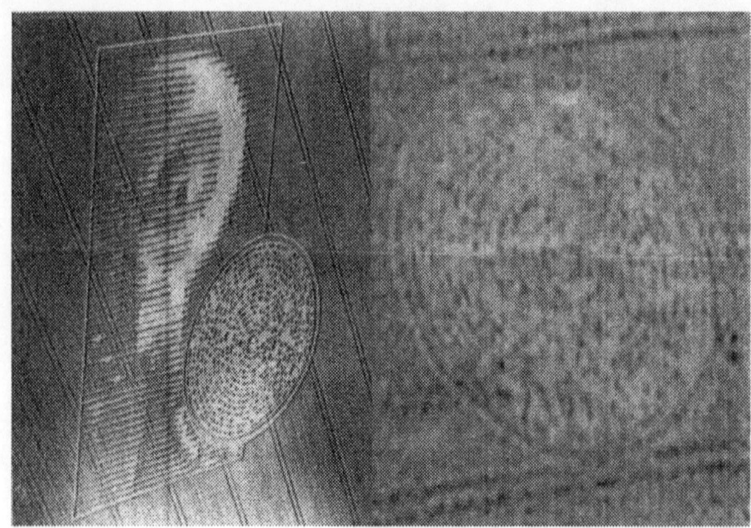

This crop circle has a coded message: "We are the good guys, not mankind!" This matches the quote by Yeshua when they called him good. "Only the Father in heaven is good," Luke 6:4. Is this proof that the aliens are the "father" and it is a plural term also. Yeshua said, "The Father and I are one." He also said we could be too!

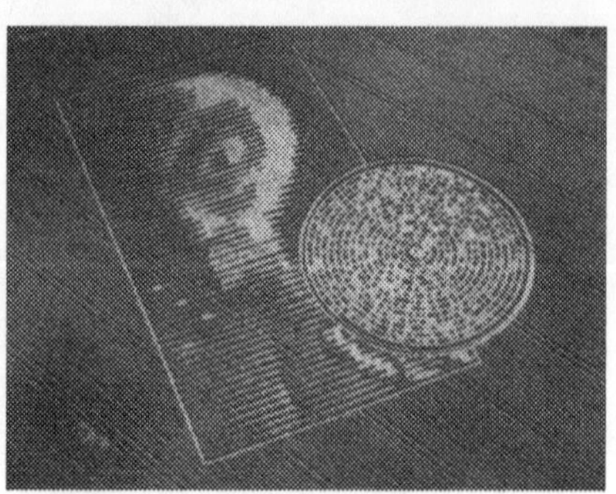

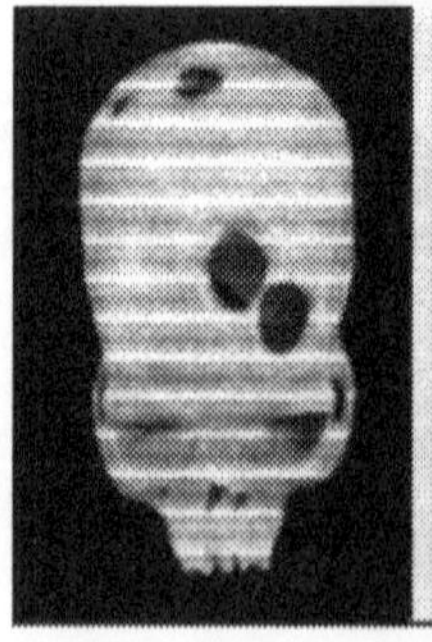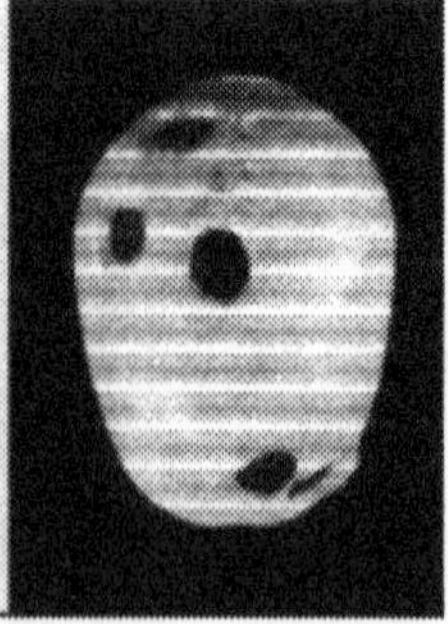

Ancient intrepanation skull! This was also universal religious practice. This could be how mental telepathy works. We are doing this today with cybernetics.

Three famous UFO incidents in the U.S. reported on the front page of each respective city's newspaper. The dates and places are on the last two. The first is Los Angeles and shows us shooting at it. It happened in Feb. 25, 1942. No wonder they don't cohabit with us. We never recovered it. Ten innocent civilians died from the shrapnel fallout!

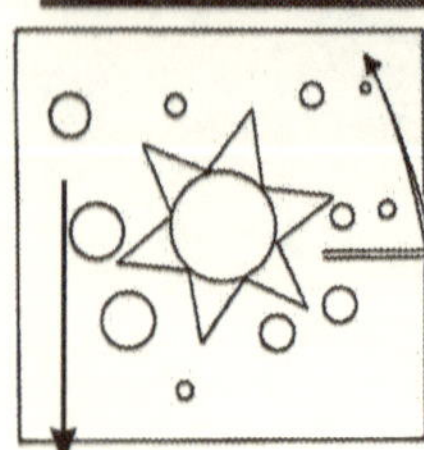

10th Planet

1. Notice cave grid looks like computer grid of space, and is flat like floating membrane. The membrane theory says space is infinite. It is a cyclical dance of creation and destruction. Also star of cave sculpture just like the Sumerian clay tablet below, and atom symbol. The clay tablet is dated circa 13000 years. The cave drawing is much older. They both show a 10th planet in our solar system. HOW?

2. The cave astronaut and gemini-looking capsule are also ancient. This is proof they existed before and supports my conclusion. Read on!

3. This is "Matching" irrefutable evidence that the ancients were communicating and space-faring people! Their absence makes it clear. Our mystery is what they look like!

4. See flying saucer in sky above astronaut!

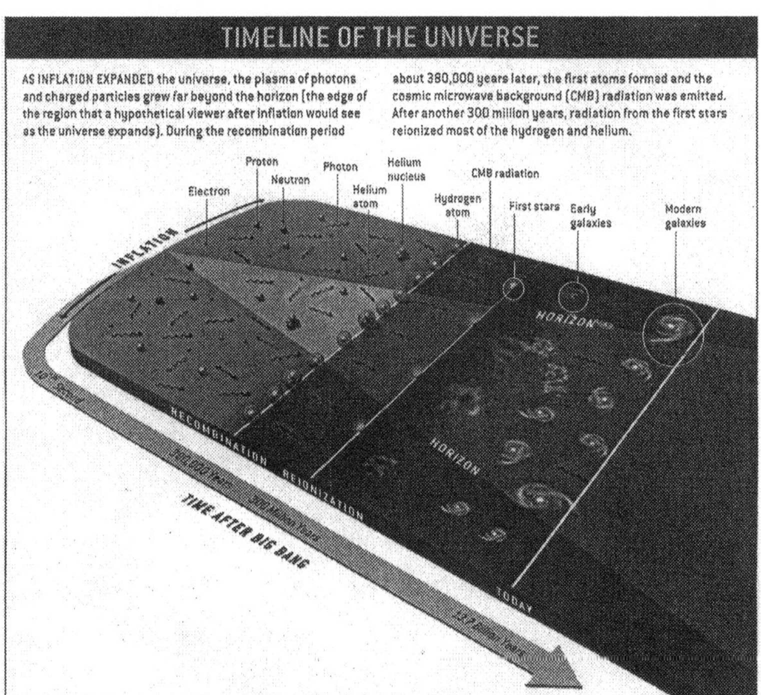

This is a perfect example of macrocosm science. The smallest parts mirror the whole. Atoms, photons, solar systems galaxies all resemble the universe itself. It is mostly space. The ancient geometry supports this theory/reality. I was amazed at how much a woman's egg looks like the sun (magnified) and when the sperm penetrates it the outer shell grows a green growth that becomes the placenta. The earth would only grow green vegetation from photon penetration. Photons look like sperm. Atoms look like suns, these look like eggs! Anyway, The problem with a beginning to our universe is that it is infinite. Only matter has a "beginning and ending". But this is an oxy-moron because atoms make matter and though one form ends it doesn't stop existing, another one just begins. This is all about image! Mind over matter and to be free of matter constraints, we must free ourselves from the matter. For space travel/freedom it is literally what we have to do. Free ourselves from the inevitable invisible eater of matter. GRAVITY! Matter itself. Does all this really matter? To be free it does. Flying is the ultimate freedom!

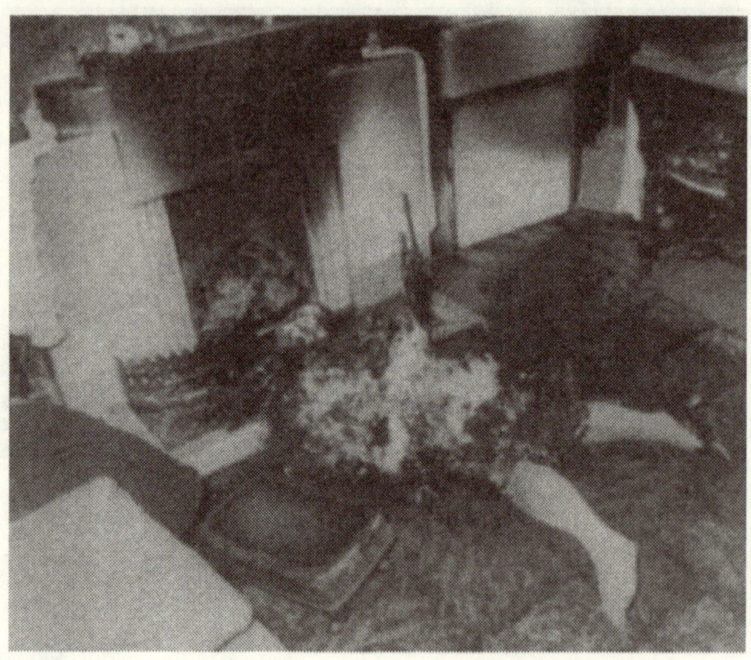

Just thought I'd throw this one in to show you proof of nuclear fusion/fission by atoms. We are made of atoms. Adams are atoms. If you think you know everything you better think again. This is a spontaneous human combustion victim. The feet are left to possibly drive home my point about flying and who we truly are! This is a perfect reason to start seeking the kingdom of Heaven! Knowledge of the Universe.

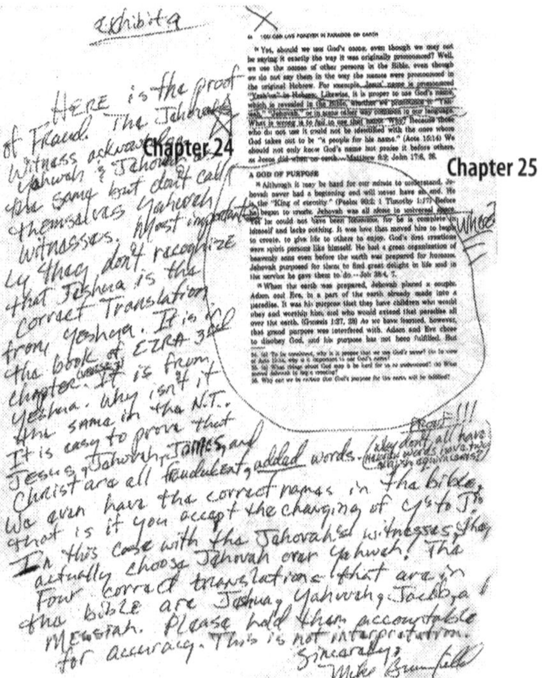

1. "Where is God?" is the $64,000 question. I thought God is omnipresent! That means everywhere like the atom! They say he's all alone in space!

2. They say he's not lonesome but he's all alone. Then they say he creates for others. That's loneliness.

ble admonishes: "If you continue showing favoritism, you are working a sin."—James 2:9.

As science and technology advance, there are many new findings and theories about the human body. It is natural to be fascinated by these concepts. Still, Christians do well to let the Bible—not human theories—guide their thinking. In all walks of life, Christians need to "make sure of all things" and "hold fast to what is fine."—1 Thessalonians 5:21.

—Awake! February 8, 2004   19

3. Finally they say he creates a heavenly organization of "spirit" sons like "himself". Why not daughters? And now they skip the fall of the angels story.

4. Last but not least. This is the proof that "religion", at least the Jews, make these angels and god "spirit" not flesh and blood. This is the ultimate cover-up. What if they come back and are the aliens? WWYD?

5. Proof that the J.W.'s discredit science! And ironically the scripture above James 2:9 makes their god a hypocrite. He has a favorite, yet forbids it. The chosen race of the Jews. No wonder people revere the Jews!

6. Finally they say the "Devil" is working through the U.N.! Don't they want a United Earth?

This is why we must prove religion's origin. The Jehovah Witnesses are not helping to make peaceful contact! They don't even realize that their answer proves mankind is religion's devil and reincarnation! (Keeps transforming).

Could I be this Michael and the war about our evil species? Notice Tibetan religion's heavenly war also involves one third being rebellions! Their Sixth Stanza reads like modern science. The final admonition is to learn the "correct" age of the "small wheel." This is the atom and us. We are atoms/adams "appearing and reappearing continuously."

Atoms are infinite!

The Gold of the Gods

stars of God: I will sit also upon the mount of the congregation, in the sides of the north."

But we also find an unmistakable reference to strife in heaven in the New Testament. Revelation xii, 7–8, reads:

> "And there was war in heaven: Michael and his angels fought against the dragon: and the dragon fought and his angels,
> "And prevailed not; neither was their place found any more in heaven."

Many of the ancient documents of mankind mention wars and battles in heaven. The Book of Dzyan, a secret doctrine, was preserved for millennia in Tibetan crypts. The original text, of which nothing is known, not even whether it still exists, was copied from generation to generation and added to by initiates. Parts of the Book of Dzyan that have been preserved circulate around the world in thousands of Sanskrit translations, and experts claim that this book contains the evolution of mankind over millions of years. The Sixth Stanza of the Book of Dzyan runs as follows: *[handwritten: Like sixth day creation in BIBLE]*

> "At the fourth (round), the sons are told to create their images, one third refuses. Two obey. The curse is pronounced . . . The older wheels rotated downward and upward. The mother's spawn filled the whole. *There were battles fought between the creators and the destroyers, and battles fought for space; the seed appearing and reappearing continuously. Make thy calculations, o disciple, if thou wouldst learn the correct age of thy small wheel."*

57

Satyr-comedy-Aristophanes: <u>Lysistrata</u>

[handwritten: Greek ~~Philosophy~~ "Sophist"]

Socrates: 469-399 BCE
    Socratic method/dialectic method
    "The unexamined life is not worth living."
Plato: 429-347 BCE, the Academy *[handwritten: (Socrates)]*
    "Until philosophers are kings or the kings and princes of the world
    have the spirit and power of philosophy...cities will never cease from
    ill, nor the human race."
Aristotle: 384-322 BCE, the Lyceum -peripatetic
    "Plato is dear, but truth is dearer."

[handwritten notes:]

Albert Einstein "I wonder if nature did not always play the same game"

Erich Von Daniken "I theorize that Alien intelligences must have been the same as homo sapiens or very much LIKE him!"

Mike Brunfield "I theorize the alien Roswell is the scientific creator of modern man/homo sapien everywhere in the universe for the "soul" purpose of working/worshipping him!"

THE
TWO WITNESSES
AND
THE
Religion
DISCOVER THIS
SHOCKING BIBLE
PROPHECY IN
REVELATION!
BY MICHAEL
WARNING: SOLVING THIS MYSTERY MAY BE HARMFUL TO YOUR HEALTH!

ALIENS
Gold
Tenth
Planet ...
PRIMITIVE MAN'S SEED
ALIEN SEED
"Amazing scientific
evidence links
the Roswell alien
with the seed of
primitive man!"
MISSING
LINK?
Read the SHOCKING new sequel
to the best-selling novel,
The Two Witnesses and
The Religion Cover-Up!
BY MICHAEL

Author's family struggle

O NE DAY, something happened to me that would change my life forever. I asked my mother, who is religious, "Where is Heaven?" She just gave me a funny look and then nervously looked up. Wow, she did just what I expected. It was the same thing that almost everyone had done before her. Most looked "UP"!

This was universal in religion. It was everywhere. I had already been polling religious people about my "SCIENTIFIC/RELIGIOUS DISCOVERY" for the past three years. I wanted to see if any of them saw this obvious scientific behavior! Most didn't. But would my mother? She was aware of my research. I anxiously waited for her answer.

"Well," she remarked with a slightly uncomfortable giggle, "I guess it's a spirit world."

I followed with the next logical question, "Why did you look up, then?"

"That's what the Jehovah's Witnesses teach, I guess," she said, puzzled-looking.

I knew what to ask next. "Does that make sense, when they're spirits (Heaven's occupants), according to your religion?" (See JW evidence.) "Spirits wouldn't need direction, would they?"

She didn't know what to say. This was a logical enough fact. So she immediately admitted that it was a puzzling contradiction. She knew I was a scientist and that I scientifically proposed to have found Yeshua/"Jesus" and Heaven. The very thing she was "looking" for. I theorized space had already been conquered with science and not religion's magic. (See my previous books and religious symbols matching science.) I based this on the lack of magic today, ancient evidence, and our current pursuits in science and space. Today's science matches ancient religion's universal themes. (See universal religious themes and today's matching science.)

I asked her, "Did you ever think it was possible the universe had another older, more scientifically advanced Earth and that they could have conquered space with flying craft, like we are now? I mean, come on, Mom, we are looking 'up' or into space for life? If this is possible they would come from up. It matches my theory and makes perfect sense."

She agreed, but said she didn't! She hadn't because her religion says there is only one Earth. They had been "TELLING HER THIS FOR FORTY-FIVE YEARS."

I told her that I did, and I think it's because I'm not allegiant to religion. Therefore, I'm able to "SEE" the historical gesture of looking up, matching today's science.

We are exploring space/going up! Moreover, all the elements of religion matched today's science, even creating. (See themes.) I asked her to think about our ability to scientifically create robots and about her God creating humans. I often wondered why people didn't question God "creating" in the first place. After all, they believe he's magical. Why bother with work, we certainly wouldn't!

But then again God is supposed to know and see everything, but can't see Adam and Eve hiding from him. Come on! I went back to my questions.

"Do they have anything in common, Mom, I mean, like a "PURPOSE"? She looked puzzled.

"What does your God and every other religion's god create man for?" I asked as lovingly as possible.

I knew she was nervous. We had been having these conversations for several years now, ever since Dad died. He wouldn't talk about these questions before; he always got angry.

"Well, you know there's only one God," she said matter-of-fact-like. She was pretty confident with her answer. "The others are pagan false gods."

"Believe me, I know you don't buy into other gods, Mom," I quickly replied. (Lord, IF SHE ONLY REALIZED LOGIC. No religion would survive, saying others are right; that's logical.) I've heard that all my life. "But it's only because you weren't born in China, right? I mean, if you were born there, you would probably be a Buddhist."

"Well, I guess you're right," she responded, rather convinced-like.

I said, "Mom, the proof's in the pudding and you're in it. The United States is the biggest bowl of pudding there is, other than Mexico. And they're really just alike. You're a white American Christian because you were raised that way. The majority of the U.S. is, Mom, because it was "CONQUERED" by white European Christians. Wouldn't you agree?"

"Well, I guess so," she said with great hesitation.

"Come on, Mom. They've even converted the Indians! It's a provable logical fact. Most Indians are Christians. That's why I said Mexico and the U.S. are just alike. But really it's worse there. They're the best example. The whole nation was brainwashed. They were damn near all converted to Catholicism. At least we had the Protestant movement here. Our so-called founders had already 'Protested' against the ONE TRUE CHURCH OF CATHOLICISM. Doesn't that one true church, which "IS" self-righteous, sound familiar to you?"

She nodded her head in agreement.

"Well, converted is really just being nice, Mom," I continued to try to explain. "Their techniques were the same then, as war-time brainwashing today. THAT'S ALSO A HISTORICAL FACT!" What our "GREAT" country did is never talked about! I wanted to ask her if she knew that *Protestant* meant *protest*, but I didn't want to confuse the issue. I knew she wasn't a seeker of historical knowledge. I really just wanted to see if she saw any scientific similarities to today's science and her religion. In fact, all religions. Because they all have the same common themes and certainly mirror today's science. This is what I wanted to figure out. How can this lack of scientific awareness among religious people still exist "TODAY" and how did it happen in our past? Well, the past is easy to understand. We weren't scientifically advanced. But it's a scientific world today! "Today" it isn't easy to understand.

She bristled at the mention of brain-washing. She knew that I thought her religion did the same thing. I had already showed her and Dad how the JW's methods matched the definition of brainwashing!

Like religion itself, they are all about the same life-or-death threat! But ironically, she still denied it, even in my Dad's absence, although she says her religion is a life-or-death matter. Denial is a symptom! Coercion, conversion, threatening is the definition of brain-washing. They always told us, it was a life-or-death matter that we come to their church. Hell, I found that most did. THAT IS WHAT RELIGION IS ABOUT, TERRORISM! (Another scientific observation: scientifically we are infinite atoms.)

Then they scared the Hell out of us with death, the devil, and his demons. (Thanks, little sister, for "making" me sleep with you.)

"But I wasn't always a Jehovah's Witness," she immediately rebutted.

"Well, we'll get to that," I said. "But let's get back to my question. What does your God's creating us and our creating robots have in common?"

She again looked perplexed. "I don't know anything about robots, but God wants us to worship him."

"This is my point exactly, Mom! They have the 'SAME PURPOSE' and you don't 'SEE' it." I laughed, because it was funny and I wanted to keep the mood light. "They are both created to serve/worship/work for their creators."

"Huh," she said with another confounded look on her face. "They do match, huh? I don't know what I was thinking. I should've gotten that!"

I thought about this being another immediate

religious contradiction to question, like creating and magic. Somebody good wanting worshipped! That's the reason I made my character Michael Jackson.

"Yeah, Mom, they do, just like the 'UP' thing. And, guess where we are going today, in science?" She just shook her head and shrugged her shoulders.

"UP, space, Mom. Isn't that amazing? Your ancient religion matches today's science, and yet, you don't 'see' it. Don't you ever think this way?"

"No, I guess I don't," she remarked flatly.

"But why?" I asked, unable to comprehend this mentality today.

"I guess I just never thought about it," she said.

"I think you said earlier why you don't. Your religion says it isn't possible."

She agreed.

"Well, there's another universal simple theme, Mom, to make scientific sense out of this. Or at least make it easier to consider. It's gold. Did you know that all religions have a gold theme and their god/angels/gods have a gold halo?"

"No, I didn't," she responded with a lot of dread in her voice. "I know we have it."

She was becoming uneasy with my knowledge! Her belief didn't provide many answers and she knew it was based on man's stories of a magic god. This really worried her because there is no magic today!

"Well, I'm going to stop right there with the themes, Mom. They're the same in every religion." (See themes.) "They all have gold, and it also matches today's science. Funny though, that religion is easily provable to be anti-wealth. And yet, we don't question the gold thing, huh."

She started to defend wealth. I find the majority do the same thing. They pervert the scripture: "Money IS the root of all evil." They made it "the love of money." The majority did this! And I ALWAYS quickly nipped it in the bud, with one scripture from Yeshua/"Jesus": "Woe to the rich and blessed are the poor!"

"Mom, I want to share one more scientific fact that I discovered about gold. Besides it being a universal religious and historical theme, too, right. Well, everyone associates it with our beginnings," (see gold chart) "and we don't scientifically question why. I don't understand why not! It seems illogical that people slaved and died for it then, huh? I mean, what was it good for? Why would a magical anti-wealth God need it? It couldn't be for art, because he certainly isn't into beauty. Religion is inner and condemns self-adornment," I said.

"Yeah, I suppose so," she remarked in a soft and weary voice. She was getting tired of the history lesson.

"Well, it doesn't make sense that it is precious to God then. It doesn't make sense that it is universal among ancient peoples. I mean, after all, we weren't global for a long time. And it's really illogical, especially, if we could rule out the knowledge of its scarceness. Right?"

She again quickly nodded her head.

I continued, "Because it isn't scarce at all. So, these COINCIDENCES/MATCHES indicate that it may have a scientific value or meaning. And guess what, Mom?" I looked deep in her eyes.

"What?" she responded instantly. She wanted to get this over with. "Don't tell me it does!"

"Yes," I blurted out with so much enthusiasm

that I think I might have caused her to pee all over herself. She nearly jumped out of her chair.

"It is important for space travel! I didn't mean to scare you, but this all matches science, Mom. We're creating, we're going up, and we use gold to do it! And last, but certainly not least, Mom, who wants to dig tunnels to get it? I don't. Guess what, Mom? We have ancient tunnel systems all over the Earth. And if we would just consider the ancient alien evidence, we could easily understand why God/aliens created us. And most importantly, why they stay away. It's obviously because THEY'RE SMALL AND FLESH BEINGS LIKE US!

"That makes a lot more sense than their loving us and staying away. I wouldn't stay away from my sons because they're bad. Hell, I can physically overcome them, like God. This can only be logical if God were too small to do it. Besides, all our Hell can't be a result of love, Mom. It's ridiculous that they're magic spirits and stay away. Hell, this would make them incapable of being hurt, if they were here! Both are ridiculous!

"And guess what, Mom, in my first book I didn't believe the universal religious story of the giants, because I hadn't seen the evidence of their existence! I was religious then and didn't really believe in anything that I didn't see. What a paradox, huh? Religion is testimony of the unseen!" I told her, laughing at myself.

"But now I have seen the truth. It exists, because the evidence does too, and it's universal! There are actual bones of giants with six fingers and toes, just like it describes them in the bible. This also matches the Roswell alien autopsy I told you about."

She never watched it. I knew why.

"And also the Egyptian drawings of the gods, which 'coincidentally' have conical-shaped bald heads. (See head-molding skulls.) The male kids are bald. Anyway, the art shows them being twice the size of men! This supports the ancient evidence I've discovered, that matches today's science and answers what they look like. I mean after all, this unseen factor of religion is what this mystery is all about. WHAT DO THEY LOOK LIKE? Not only do we have the giant thing, universal religious baldness, and the alien smallness, but the 'FALL OF THE ANGELS' is what I theorize this is all about," I said in utter amazement at the world's not seeing this for what it is.

"Power through beauty of the Flesh! Our extreme makeover is us." That was it. She didn't buy the alien thing. I don't think she will. I never even mentioned the big eye connection of the Egyptians and everywhere else. I knew nothing would help.

Huh, she never saw any God, angel, devil, demon, or giant, yet believed in them. But did she, really? I hadn't when I was religious either. She was religious and really didn't buy anything, like I used to be. She was not open to new/old evidence. I would soon discover her own addiction to beauty of the flesh, like mine. And we all have déjà vu! Think about it! Destiny IS a universal theme. We're all here aren't we?

I asked if she thought the Jehovah's Witnesses were the only ones who are right. She did. I asked her if she knew who started it and when it was founded. SHE DID NOT KNOW! I asked if she would believe any man who said he knew where Heaven was. She wouldn't. I told her she already did. She looked confused. I plainly stated the obvious. "You believed a Jehovah's Witness, didn't you, because you are one."

"Well, I checked out their answers in the Bible and they matched." I was surprised. I had never seen her do this. I had never seen her use any other Bible than the JWs. So, I jumped at this new opportunity.

"Who told you these answers and which Bible did you use? Was it the King James Version, which is the first English Bible? And more importantly, do you know who wrote the Bible?"

She said God did, just like most other Christians, Moslems, and Jews. I told her it is a provable scientific fact that men did. I really just wanted to know the scientific answer, which was the historical date that it was written.

She knew what I wanted, but tried to explain that God really wrote it. "Because he told them what to write."

I told her that they all say this, even today. Heck, just watch church on television. She went to one. God's talking to them all, even the President!

"So, what makes them different from me, Mom? Would you believe me if I said that?"

She shrugged her shoulders. I knew she wouldn't believe me. I didn't press. I had asked her before.

My struggle is chronicled in the previous three books. (See reviews.) She would think I'm crazy, like the rest of the world. Hell, I'd think I was crazy! The whole world thinks it's crazy. And one thing's for sure, if anybody says that God told them to kill, they're crazy! (See evidence of mothers killing for this reason!) And the Bible is full of this! God kills his own innocent children of Sodom and Gomorrah. This is crazy. We wouldn't allow a parent to kill a child just because he disobeyed! Forget asking them why he didn't make the world perfect and about the sick fact that he demands to be worshipped. I had already asked her this a long time ago. She, too, thinks a human wanting to be worshipped is a sickness and would make the world perfect, if she could. But she didn't "SEE" it with god!

Anyway, she didn't know when the Bible was written and didn't know who wrote it! She didn't really even have a clue when the word/concept God came into being. (See fossil timeline. We can prove when religion started with science.) This was my point! How could someone feel so strongly about something that they hadn't even proven to exist? It's easy, tradition! She didn't know anything about the other religions either, except what the JWs told her. And she had already humbly admitted that she was a Christian because she was raised one. And even if she wasn't, she admitted the likelihood of her becoming one is extremely high, just because the majority of our country is CHRISTIAN.

This lack of awareness doesn't happen only with traditional religious followers. Even people who aren't raised religious, but become so, seem to exhibit this lack of scientific awareness about themselves. (Even though God is everywhere, in our currency, schools, courts, money, politics, and mainstream society!) They seem unsure of why they believe so strongly in God and why they converted when they weren't taught it. It's obvious they don't "SEE" it because they are it: religious.

And the best evidence of their religious disease is their strong denial of this possibility. This angry refusal to admit the obvious scientific facts perplexes me. Why are we so prone to resisting self-criticism. I think it's all hormonal. We're to sexual to have our level of intelligence. It seems as if I am "fighting a losing battle," trying to share my theories with religious people. But, I would at least think that knowing God's beginning would take first priority. And if they don't know this, at least admit they could be a victim of religious societal peer-pressure. (Please remember that I have evidence to prove the existence of primitive man's god. He doesn't look like us and isn't magical. I never say that he doesn't exist!) Especially, if they're so emphatic that God does exist and yet can't make him show or prove his magic! And it really kills me when they finally use nature as proof, because nature proves science, not magic. Nature grows! (another scientific observation of universal religious behavior) Why can't religious people see this contradiction?!

NATURE PROVES SCIENCE, NOT MAGIC! I know why, though. It is traditional brain-washing, when an individual accepts a parent's or society's beliefs and doesn't question it. That's what my first book is about. I suffered the wrath of God/Dad, trying to show them the definition of brain-washed followers and that they fit its description. They knew absolutely no scientific facts about God/religion's beginnings. This is the best evidence to prove this possibility. It is the first symptom! Religion, sect, denomination, CULT are all one and the same! (See definition.) They think they're right and use life/death/punishment/reward/TERROR as a sales pitch/tool to get you to join them. Their motive is GROWTH! Even though "FEW" is the "KNOWN OUT-COME"!

My parents saw that others could be religious-ly brain-washed, but refused to accept this possi-bility for themselves! This seem to be universal among religious people. They even went to yearly assemblies that bragged about their growth! Funny, though, because Yeshua/"Jesus" said few will en-ter! No way! Were these people brain-dead? That's how we portray brain-washed victims. They aren't in their "right" mind. Their normal one "left." I'm thankful they classify me as a liberal left-winger!

Well, enough of this. I knew this discussion was going nowhere. I had done the brain-washing thing many times before, with them and plenty of people at my book-signings. And many, and I do mean many, attacked me. Supposedly loving par-ents turned into devils right in front of their children. It was sad. They wanted to save me at first, but kill me at the end. So, they just told me that I was going straight to Hell. They didn't do this with tears either, but anger. I think that they really would've enjoyed killing me themselves, but they held off for the kids' sake.

Thank God, I mean aliens, for kids. I even got death threats from preachers and had to go to the police. The JWs literally threw me out of their church. Yeah, it's true. Six to eight of them did it as I cried out, "Please help me, I come in peace." Nobody moved. It was awful what the children had to see. (Again, it's in my first book.) I can only hope the memory fades with time and that they won't experience it themselves.

It's a terrible thing to have your religious leaders attack you. Just read the Gospels or watch "Passion of the Christ." I cried and turned it off. They brutally killed Yeshua/"Jesus." I was lucky. "Okay," I said with a little disbelief at what was happening. I didn't want to go there again. You can't cure people of this. You can only provide the evidence to prove it and if they don't get it, they won't get it. They are RELIGIOUSLY BRAINWASHED! I want to say here and now that following is the disease. I also saw crop circle followers want to kill hoaxers! Following perverts the mind and turns it into a lover of itself. I had enough of this! So I went back to my point.

Ultimately though, I wanted to know what it would take to get her to think scientifically. I wanted to know what it would take to make her leave the JWs! (Deep down, I already knew!) But first, I had to finish my point.

"What 'false' scripture of your Dad's did the 'MAN' sell you on for the Jehovah's Witnesses, Mom?" I used quotes with the *man* word. She got my point. "That is what you said, made you believe him, I mean them, right?" I was ribbing her about this obvious contradiction. "I mean, you did say that earlier, didn't you?" I kind of laughed, but didn't mean any harm.

"Well," she again quickly rebutted, a little too seriously for my liking. I knew this was about to come to an end. "I believed what he showed me in the Bible and not him," she said. I didn't interrupt her. I loved her so much.

Besides, I really wanted to ask "THE ULTIMATE QUESTION"! (WHY DON'T THEY CONTACT US OPEN-

LY? THIS IS KNOWN AS FERMI'S PARADOX. THERE ARE ONLY TWO LOGICAL ANSWERS. THEY DON'T EXIST OR WE'RE NOT A 'GOOD' THING. THE LATTER IS OBVIOUS, AND THEIR PURPOSE FOR OUR CREATION IS TOO: WORK FOR THEM/WORSHIP THEM! THIS IS ALSO UNIVERSAL; SEE THEMES.)

She continued to tell me that "brother Reed" from the church had come to her door. "So, factually, you did believe another man's truth." I have always remembered his soft demeanor. No wonder she believed him. He was the polar opposite of what she was used to. She looked aggravated! She tried to answer, but I knew what she was going to say.

"All right, I know you're getting annoyed at me. So, what was it that made you believe him, Mom?" (Although she did just say that she wouldn't believe any man.)

She went on, only more seriously this time. I knew she wasn't aggravated, though; she was hurting. I could feel her pain! It was terrible. Damn religion!

To better quote my feelings: "GOD DAMN THE PREACHER/PUSHER MAN" and his guilt trip! (NI-

ETZSCHE SAID RELIGION IS A DRUG, AND I LIKE THE REBELLIOUS SONG! IT'S ABOUT TIME WE OPENLY QUESTION THEM.)

She went on. "Well," she said slowly and with great care, "he showed us that Hell didn't exist. And he came along right after the death of my little girl. I needed answers."

Now, I understood perfectly how her transition took place. She went from the Hellfire-and-brimstone Baptist of her tyrant father to my Dad's religion. He was a tyrant, also, but this all made perfect sense now. I wasn't about to ask where he showed her this. It was like all the other scriptures that they fraudulently changed. (See JW fraud evidence.)

I showed her and Dad many changes in my first book. All religions claim God is everything (omnipresent), but they made him a person separate from everything. It is a universal theme. They even say that he was "somewhere" in the universe in the beginning. Come on! They made the scripture "ye are god's" into "ye are as gods." Jesus was killed for saying he was God and that we are too. This is easy to prove. Use the global concordance on the Internet or get one.

Ironically, the only name that is memorialized by their God is "I am." This means that we are all gods. All this is provable, like the false name of Jehovah, James, and Jesus. EVEN THE NAME OF THEIR CHURCH IS FALSE! It is Yahweh, because we have Y's in our language! (See JW fraud evidence.)

Anyway, I wasn't about to say anything else. I saw tears welling up in her eyes, and my brother Brian (Jeff in the other books.) walked in. He had been listening. I didn't want to hurt her. It was time to stop! He went straight to her and hugged her. I felt like an asshole. No, I am one! I never should've discussed this again. (Read my first book!) I already knew the answer to my ultimate question. Mom had already told me, as well as Dad, what it would take to make them leave the JWs. They said provable false teachings. Well, Dad went to his death-bed without ever giving anything a look. In spite of all my help, which made it easier. So, it wasn't about its being difficult to prove. And it was perfectly clear that Mom would, too, which was fine by me.

But the question really tugged at my mind. Would she ever accept new scientific evidence? I held my ground and didn't say a word. I wasn't going to ask her anything else!

"Mike, dammit," Brian said. "You know why she became a JW!" he angrily hollered out. "Brother Reed consoled her and it was comforting."

Mom agreed.

"But didn't Dad's family practice with them, Mom?" There I went again. But Brian quickly put me in check.

"Yes, goddammit," Brian bellowed out again. "You know that."

She got on to him and said it was all right.

"Yes," she said, "but that isn't why I chose them. My Dad's religion wasn't able to answer my questions. They taught Hell, and the JWs didn't."

This was obviously the real reason. And who could blame her? Besides, my Dad ruled and her Dad scared her to death, too. POOR MOM, SHE WAS TERRORIZED BY THEM AND RELIGION! That was bad enough, let alone losing a child. And now she's lost two. I thought about my brother David (his name was Sam in my last book), who committed suicide a couple of years ago, and Nancy.

I wanted to dedicate this to him, Nancy, and most importantly, Mom. I didn't want her to hurt anymore. I have to admit, that Yeshua/"Jesus" taught Hell and, to me, that is here. This was it! The JWs glorified man, and they had Mom hook, line, and sinker. I found that this was also universal among religious people today. I didn't want to hurt anybody else, especially Mom. I hated the Two Witnesses scripture in Revelation. They tortured people with the answer about us. With them, the mystery of God, which is man, is finished. Well, I was finished! I didn't know if I am one of them or not, but I certainly knew one thing for sure: I didn't want to torture people, but I was.

That was eerie enough, let alone my name being Michael. He reveals the angels at the end of our mystery, and we still don't know what they look like! THAT IS WHAT THE MYSTERY IS! IT'S OBVIOUSLY WHY THEY DON'T SHOW AS WELL! The coincidences really freaked me out. I got goose bumps every time I thought about it. I had them now. It was time to go.

I finally stated that I didn't think anyone would believe Yeshua/"Jesus" when he comes. She quickly said he already came in 1914, "invisibly." I didn't want to further this anymore. How could the JWs prove this, if he's invisible? Or for that matter, how could anyone else disprove it! Even worse, how could they sell such a ridiculous "truth"? Man, did they ever have a successful sales plan. No Hell and everything else is "spirit"!

I explained to them both that all religions believe in a spirit world. "And, no offense intended, but I find no difference in yours and theirs. Hell, the rest look up, too!" I got up to leave. I had definitely had enough. I didn't want to discuss this anymore. I loved her too much!

She tried to explain some differences between her religion and theirs, but couldn't. I was really kind of taken aback by her next sentence. She started explaining that they were the only ones who acknowledge the real name of "Jesus." I knew what name she was going to say. (See scripture evidence.)

I had heard it all my life. It was mine: Michael. "Mom, I love you, but do you think it could be me?" I left myself wide open for disappointment. But not really, for I already knew the answer.

She hesitated and said "No." But my brother chimed in.

"Mom, that's really kind of sad, because that's the problem with religion. They won't even believe their own children. They won't believe anything you show them."

Then she said weakly, "Well I suppose so. I guess you could be him." She started to say something else. "But. . . ."

I stopped her. "Mom, it's okay. Please, don't worry about it. It's all right, because I'm used to it by now. Don't worry about anything. Hell, I think we exist forever, like science says energy/the atom does. I only wish you did. Because, I promise, you will see Nancy again and I can't wait. I love you so much. You of all people deserve it. You're the best Mom a man could wish for."

I immediately went over and kissed her. Brian quickly agreed and joined in for a great group hug. It was beautiful. I knew she didn't think I could be "MI-CHAEL," but I didn't really get offended. It wasn't her fault. It was religion's. I hugged her and laughed.

"What if I could levitate, though, would that prove it to you?" I think I scared her. She shrugged her shoulders sheepishly and started to stammer for an answer. I read her mind. I knew that would really freak her out. She didn't know what to say. I knew what it would take. And it wasn't magic. Not for believers in evil spirits, anyway. And the majority (if not all) believed in that, too! I couldn't win for already losing! When it came to religion, I was a loser. "IT WAS ALREADY WRITTEN!"

I thought about the reality of this. The majority of the Earth is religious and "FEW" are not! Then, I suddenly realized that the scripture "believe no man that comes in my name" pretty much signed, sealed, and delivered it. And if that didn't do it then the scripture telling us not to believe those coming and performing "MIRACLES," would. What if these miracles were today's SCIENCE?

I didn't give up. I continuously asked others about Heaven. They all looked up, but said it was a spirit world! Surprisingly, some even knew the scripture about his return. But, most didn't get the spirit contradiction. He was coming just like he left, "on the clouds!" It didn't really matter, because most wouldn't believe it anyway. It was already destined, which is a universal teaching.

Few will enter. This fact alone ought to wake up followers of any large religion! As I was leaving, I thought about the ultimate question that I wanted to ask Mom. I decided to ask Brian instead. "Brian, what will it take for religious people to consider new scientific evidence?"

Brian simply said, "Nothing. They won't!"

We all just laughed as I walked away. But deep down, I knew some would believe the evidence/me. It would take a lot of humility, and Mom has that. More than anyone else, I know that seeing/contact is the ultimate believing test! The evidence will speak for itself. Ultimately, it always has and always "WILL!" Get my point? It exists now! We are the infinite mystery, because we are scientifically flawed! She would see it with her own eyes. We all will. FEW DO NOW!

She finally believes me. But would she want the torturous truth about ourselves? Well, that's another story, the ending. So, please enjoy and read on!

Introduction

RELIGION AND science both say that life/mankind/God exist "somewhere" in the universe. (See JW evidence of fraud.) But where? Scientifically, this answer is simple. It's "Up" or on another planet. Either way, they are one and the same, as you have to go "up" to reach another planet. This logic holds true not only with today's science, but with all ancient religions! They even agree that space is ultimately the safest place to live and not a planet! Heaven is religion's home. As scientists, we are finally catching "up" to religion's/history's irrefutable universal beginning. Religion is history! (See man's timeline.) Heaven is up, to all primitive people, and still is, in every religion's writings today.

Even though this answer is overwhelmingly

"up," it has universally become a spirit realm today. How did this happen and why does it exist, in lieu of all this evidence? This age-old question still applies: "Where is Heaven?" Why? It's "easy" to "see" why now. Ironically, I didn't know this happened until I started my research back in 1989. Why not?

Obviously, I hadn't really "looked" before then. But, how could I have not looked when I had gone to church all my life. I even went door to door, "MINISTERING ANSWERS" at the tender age of twelve! Well, the evidence is clear and so is the reason why. I was the blind following the blind. I had been following my parents' religious tradition. When I finally did begin to search, I tried to remember what my answer was then. I couldn't remember! Wow, I must have been just like a brain-washed moonie child/zombie! I had to accept the obvious scientific facts about myself or I wouldn't get better. I wanted to get better. So, I started at its beginning and discovered that religion is history. I scientifically "researched" history. (See my first book.)

I did this with complete humility, because I was ignorant of it. Even though I had a degree and majored in history! Wow, they are one and the same.

This is why I put our timeline chart on the very first page. OUR MYSTERY IS EASY TO PINPOINT! The timeline shows just how it happened! Something took place that caused a MISSING LINK in the fossil record. It's clear that primitive man's head is like an ape's. He also evolved for millions of years, without any advance in knowledge. (Again, see chart.) Then we came along and the mystery/missing link began (on this Earth anyway!) I theorize that primitive man's god is flesh and blood, because "THE UP EVIDENCE RULES OUT A SPIRIT OR INTERDIMENSIONAL BEING." He would also have a large head, due to his intelligence. This event clearly shows a short history for a new, big-headed *homo sapiens*/us. We not only jumped a skull size, but we suddenly became religious and began to bury our dead. If you mixed a big head species with a small head species, it would cause this missing link mystery—especially if their creation was uncontrollable and they had to leave. (Head molding/enlargement and trepanation/skull drilling followed. This evidence is important for my conclusion.)

From then on, stories of a god creator were passed down to this very day. This god creator is

"FROM THE SKY." It is the foundation of every ancient society, and "HE" has always been "CONNECTED TO GOLD." The scripture "Heaven's streets are paved in gold" became the driving force, not only in Judaism but every economy. Why would god revere gold? This really fueled my curiosity and drive to solve our mystery. In their absence, the gold halo became the universal symbol of god. It was placed above his head, "UP", when he left. "HIS" absence is obviously what our mystery is about.

We wouldn't have it if they were here! Anyway, this event/"our creation" produced a very simple clue. Up and the gold halo were connected! I had learned gold is crucial for space travel/exploration, and religion's "purpose"/will. It suddenly made sense! See Genesis Project evidence. Maybe it's the design of their fiery chariots. I now have read and discovered many religious descriptions of the same, from the Hindu vimanas to tribal religion's flying ships that shimmered like gold. I had seen a flying saucer like many others and we have many, many ancient artworks of them. We even have a photo of JOHNNY CASH WITH ONE ABOVE HIS HEAD! FOR "GOD'S" SAKE WHY DON'T WE EXAMINE THIS AND

LET THE EVIDENCE SPEAK FOR ITSELF! I mean, after all, seeing is believing! But I knew why, just like Erich Von Daniken. Priests would lose their power! (See his quote.) I wasn't aware of all this, because I had been raised a Jehovah's Witness.

It was started in 1897 by an eighteen-year-old boy, and I'm sure my Mom wouldn't believe him now! Man, was I ever a lazy seeker and a great follower, then. I never even "researched" the word *God*, which I believed so much in. Why hadn't I? You'd think that this would be the first thing I would've done. But, I never saw my parents do it. I believed Heaven to be a spirit realm, just like them and the rest of the world. This was why I didn't get it: "WORLD-WIDE" peer pressure! I read over this word "up" at least a thousand times, but never got it. I didn't get it for a long time. I guess it was because my "older" buddy (the other witness of the first book) "IS" a big believer in spirits. He was also raised a Christian and had an out-of-body experience. I remember well how his O.B.E. had a profound effect on me. It was definitely strange, like many other universal mysteries that I started to discover. I wasn't aware of it and yet people had them all over the Earth! But how could this be? Now I knew why! I HAD BEEN RELIGIOUSLY BRAIN-WASHED!

I never thought about our scientific future. If I had, then the world around me gave plenty of evidence that scientific truth is stranger than fiction. This is a FACT that is extremely obvious today! Especially in lieu of "EXTREME MAKEOVER"! Anyway, these O.B.E.s were commonly called near-death experiences. This coming "up" out of the body intrigued me. Was it connected to Heaven's "upward" direction and if so, how? I wanted to know more! And why didn't I know about this "OBVIOUS" flip-flop with Heaven's origin, anyway? After all, we were looking at other religions and using a concordance for the Bible. It was full of references to heaven being "UP." I guess it was because of my buddy's persistent belief in the spirit world that we didn't look "UP"! But, then something happened to me. We began to try and achieve an O.B.E. through the Jewish Mystery (Indian Spirit Quest/TM). We figured this must be the way to be born again "of the spirit," according to "Jesus"/Yeshua. It fit the description of his prayer method to a tee. He prayed in secret, sitting. We found this to be a universal religious practice. It was especially obvious here, where sitting Indian-style was practiced in school. The first attempt took everything I could muster up. It took a lot of courage to conquer my ingrained fear of the "Spirit" world. My parents still believe in the devil and demons! What's even worse is that my buddy did, too. Well, I had conquered my fear of the JWs' condemnation. So, I knew, that I could do this! I got angry at myself for getting so afraid and I did it! And guess what happened? Nothing! I even grew comfortable with it and was really getting good at achieving the small, "still" voice. I was so relieved! I got so comfortable that we tried even harder and longer to make contact! Yes, my buddy wanted to make contact. I was nervous. We sat for hours.

Then it happened! I started to remember my alien contact encounter. I didn't want to remember this! It scared the crap out of me. It was hideously ugly ! I was only six when it happened, and, worse yet, it happened at night! I was so young and afraid of the dark. My parents had really brain-washed me that the demon and his devils are always trying to get me (win my soul?) But, even though it was "ugly" and I was definitely freaked out, something "good" happened that fateful night. It was something that would change my life forever, just like my buddy's O.B.E. and people's N.D.E. Nothing happened! I lived!

Well, at least I thought that nothing happened. Anyway, I lived on. And believe me, this made me ecstatic, just like them! It's a shame that it takes facing death for the sexual mind to become an intellectual one! More proof that we are sexually flawed due to this scientific mixing. I thought Kurt Russell said it best: "We think too much about SEX!" And at "FACE VALUE," nothing did happen that night. It took place over the next twenty-five years. I continuously witnessed our addiction to beauty of the flesh/sex, over and over again. I took up for the "ugly" schoolkids, the poor, and the handicapped. I saw beauty's unfair POWER and cruel nature, destructive to everyone. And, I had fallen prey to it as well! I had viciously used women for sex. My first wife will testify to that. I want her to know that I AM an asshole and AM deeply sorry. She deserved better than me. I am tortured with regret. Could I have been this alien? Is this why people have O.B.E.s, N.D.E.s, and déjà vu? I suddenly realized that I hadn't ever given it much thought until this moment. I guess it was a nightmare and I wanted to forget. But, in the back of my mind I never forgot. (Had I been mentally altered, then?) I just never really got "it," until now. The message that is. The "NOW"/"STILL VOICE" was what made it surface so vividly. Does the brain wavelength activate the "CHIP"? (See nanotechnology evidence.) Did I have a chip? The alien had "telepathically" (our brain's voice is digital, one language) told me that we are them, addicted to the awful scientific creation of mankind. Mankind is the evil of the universe, because we perceive and are controlled by outward beauty. I was addicted to outward beauty and my own power of it. It told me I was him in a strange flesh that isn't natural and would never exist without scientific creation. I knew this deep down and was trying to control it. I had already hurt enough people and I had been hurt. I also had déjà vu! Worse yet, I was seeing evidence of this possibility. My brother Terry recently bought a liger! It was half lion and half tiger. My brother is the greatest. Thank you. Terry!

Well, as a result of this memory, I began to theorize that the universe was already conquered by them. I reached this conclusion first and foremost because of this event and the ancient evidence I began to find. Today's weird science didn't hurt either. They are obviously more scientifically advanced than us. They had bigger heads, weren't pretty, and they all looked the same! This is self- explanatory! There's no reason for war/division! Besides, it would be ridiculous to think that some other Earth isn't much older than ours. We could easily achieve this same feat within the next thousand years. Come on! (But we won't, because we don't want to look the same. This is my mother's paradox at the end. And most importantly, "OUR DESTINY"!) I mean after all, let's face it, we are still scientifically advancing. They must've not only conquered space but created us to worship/work for them.

Religion's story doesn't make sense, that they love us and stay away. It's perfectly clear why we were created! How can they cover this up, like heaven's location? (See first book's title.) Their predestined will/god's plan sounds just like a scientific experiment, one where the experimentee is being "used" for the good of the universe. They must need our services in spite of our evil/self-destructive nature. Religion is all about "SERVING"/working for others! According to it we are just that! Our mystery is obviously just "collateral damage." We must be the "ends to the mean," or, better said, "means to the end." We are mean!

This made sense to me. Especially since we are creating robots to work for us! The movie *I, Robot* epitomizes the evil nature of differences among intelligent/SERVING beings. *Logan's Run* epitomized a scientific addiction to beauty and youth thirty years ago! It was a science fiction movie from my childhood that had a huge and lasting impact on me. They transplant faces, something that's actually happening now! Wow, does this ever drive the "INNER MESSAGE OF RELIGION AND DÉJÀ VU" home. I did backslide or have frequent brain-death, like I told you with my first wife's story. I still do. I don't think our "MOVIES" are a coincidence! I have to accept science and religion. They both agree that nothing is new under the sun! I also have to believe this, because we don't have any proof of a spirit being. And it doesn't make sense that a spirit being created a physical world! I and the rest of the world are proof that we are all addicted to a flawed scientific reality.

I started telling my buddy about my experience and obviously repressed memories. I theorized that the aliens are the angels of the Bible. (See universal evidence of one-third being cast out of Heaven/the fall in war between gods. It is Michael's war!) I told him that they had obviously done this for "outward" power, because they all looked the same. It's logical, and they're all equal in religion's Heaven, just like the aliens are here. IT MATCHES! Just look at Easter Island heads! They all look the same! They even "FALL" prey to their "LUST FOR POWER."

It's obvious that sex and variety is our problem; maybe it's theirs, too! Beauty indisputably gives us power over one another! It's painfully obvious that "We"/mankind could never last long enough to conquer space because of this. Anyway, my buddy resisted any notion of my theory and even laughed wildly, like it was ridiculous. Ironically, he did this in spite of his anything-is-possible attitude and belief in "MAGIC." Oh, yeah, sex, too! Man, is he brain-washed! Hell, his magic world could do far greater. He absolutely refused to consider my scientific scenario. He stood fast in his belief of spirits. I was shocked!

But, then again, everybody did the same thing. I asked them why they laughed at my theory. After all, science supports this reality in our very own near future. Furthermore, I told him and the rest of them that their religious God is just like the Santa Claus story. He has the same characteristics, up and away, not to be found! Their god "CREATED US TO TILL THE GROUND AND WORSHIP HIM"; he didn't blink or think us! And furthermore, he repented immediately for doing it.

As a matter of fact, the evidence clearly supports my reality instead of theirs. There isn't any blinking thinking magic today, and the ancient artworks speak for themselves. I showed him and my family these discoveries, but they didn't care and were pretty cruel, to boot! Most quickly told me that I better just trust in God, because science was doing enough harm to the world as it is. (Again see JW fraud anti-science evidence.) Yet, they used science to disprove Santa! No way.

They even have the same description, Santa and God. What? Why don't they use science to try and prove God, since they use it to disprove Santa? They must, or it's hypocritical! They didn't care, but they wouldn't give up science, either. Can't they see that religious war is ravaging our planet? It's on the evening news every day. I had to accept the horrifying reality around me. They don't and won't challenge religion because they are religious followers, not Santa followers!

Wow, my "older" buddy and almost everyone I know was religiously brainwashed. And I mean bad. I couldn't shake it, not even with the simplest evidence facing mankind today. HEAVEN IS UP! UP would become part of the first book's title, and really is what my search was all about.

"Where is Heaven?" How can the world not know this answer? Religion's Upness is everywhere, and we are going up! But, then again, I know how. I was almost kept brainwashed by my "older" buddy. It's called tradition/religion, and it rules planet Earth with a ferocious, vengeful pride! Not "honoring" our forefathers' traditions is breaking society's most-sacred global taboo! That's why this struggle, science versus religion, continues and is infinite. Breaking it brings unwanted attention! This proves that mankind is incurable, even in the face of ancient religion's hard evidence, like "UP," GOLD, and CREATION, all of which are key components of our own space exploration! This scientifically MATCHES!

This is why we are a mystery. We are an unstoppable, flawed scientific creation that is in love with its own creation. We are the "STRANGE FLESH," the infinite mystery, that is "DESTINED" to be the same! Our mystery started when we became globally wicked and will end (on this Earth) as such.

We are globally wicked now. We are nuclear and uncontrollable! NOW, LET'S SOLVE THIS MYSTERY. PLEASE? I'M BEGGING, FOR OUR CHILDREN'S SAKE! Again, here are the historical and scientific facts about mankind! If primitive man is on a planet when we land there, he will say we came from up. All religions do! If we could scientifically manipulate him to work/worship for us, we would, because it is logical. Again, they do! It is cost-prohibitive to carry a workforce in space and not possible even in our near-future. The majority of our Earth is reli gious and does this very thing: worship God! If we wanted to maximize production from this creation, we would make him more intelligent and competitive through variety. We have it!

Mankind is intelligent and varied, causing us to be the most competitive creatures in the universe! This would be done with DNA. Ancient man gave us the ancient AMA symbol, and it matches today's DNA! (See matching symbols! Intertwined serpent art is in every culture, like the spiral, which looks like a galaxy/solar system and again supports their being space travelers!) If this intellectually enhanced man (now modern) got out of control and caused us to leave, this would start their mystery/religion and create a missing link in the fossil record. We would also control this creation, through a non-physical scientific contact like holograms or medical abductions.

We have a universal spirit teaching in religion, are a mystery due to a missing link in our fossil record, and have an abduction alien phenomenon! (See fossil/timeline chart.) We would also have religious stories of magic that mirror today's science. We have this, with our creation of the liger, being the most like ourselves! (See religion and science comparison.) This mystery would be religions' "FALL," since we live "UP" in spacecraft. Religions all have it! If gold were important for space exploration, it would be proven by the same eventual historical outcome.

It is, and we are conquering space with it! It would also be the reason for his creation, and man's mystery would be rooted in gold. It is, and the Bible even says that "Adam was created to till the ground!" If gold were the crucial element to achieve space travel, because it protected them and their flying spacecraft/saucers, God's symbol would be gold and resemble our craft. Voilà, it does! (See aborigine cave painting of saucer, alien, and gold halo going up! And see also the gold sphere evidence from Turkey, eight thousand years old.) NASA's symbol is even a halo with a rocket going through it! However, we are currently working on saucer-shaped spacecraft. There is ancient evidence of these future spacecraft world-wide! (See covers and pictures.) We recovered one, in 1947, at Roswell, New Mexico. (See newspaper evidence.) We also recovered bodies that matched ancient artworks. (See alien autopsy.)

This future craft will solve our anti-gravity problems in space and explain the weird motion behavior of these sightings today. It spins to create this ability. (See pictures and evidence.) This symbol would also support the literal direction of where we came from, up! Again, man's universal religious creator/god has a GOLD halo above his head! THIS ALL MATCHES! If man's creation was a bad thing, but scientifically couldn't be stopped, then we would forever be an infinite mystery.

Mankind is still a mystery! Our separation and return would always be called his religious mystery/will/destiny or predestined plan. IT IS! This plan would be carried out for the sole reason of ensuring the propagation of our space-faring species (Heaven). MULTIPLYING IS THE CENTRAL THEME OF RELIGION AND SCIENCE! Since we can't stop their self-destructive behavior, we'd always have to return and save the Earth from them. All religions have this second-coming story! IT IS THE ATLANTIS STORY OF GLOBAL MATERIAL DESTRUCTION! THIS MYSTERIOUS SPECIES would develop quickly, have a missing link in their fossil record, and most likely have a large head. We have these, especially the large head; just ask a doctor or woman giving birth! (Again, see fossil chart.)

Logic dictates that their creators would have large heads, small frail bodies, and their color would be extremely white-looking from living in spaceships! Again, there's no way this can be a coincidence. This can't be a coincidence! Our heads are too large, and we have a missing link in the fossil record! (See fossil timeline.) We also have evidence of flying saucers, one universal depiction of a small-bodied/large-headed/big-eyed alien presence with primitive man, and are on the threshold of conquering space ourselves. This is our current situation!

Oh my God, uh, I mean alien! Well, I guess that's what I'm asking everyone. Could the God of primitive man be this ancient alien? The evidence matches this reality! Could we be them? I knew Mom wouldn't want to be, but what about everybody else? I didn't want to be ugly. "Jesus"/Yeshua's message and all religious stories are inner! Religion is anti-materialism and all about the inner! Unbelievable! Why don't we "see" this SIMPLE TRUTH

ABOUT OURSELVES? But, then again, by now we all know why. Religion! Our recorded history is dominated by the Jewish religious calendar of six thousand years and, yes, they make man good. However, they aren't the earliest.

We are digging up pre-flood evidence everywhere. (See mother-goddess statues.) They both show head abnormalities similar to aliens. This was a time when they were with these beings from the heavens. The actual biblical timeline of the Jews is seven thousand years and is Sumerian, which is older. One thousand years of the Jewish calendar is for the millennium of peace. It is yet to come. They are almost at the six thousand mark. (I will look up their actual year now.) That's what my final story is about, the scientific future of peace! Anyway, they trace their history back to the "first" man, Adam, who was created by God. But where did their God come from and what does he look like? Is he just like us?

We are made in His image! Genesis is an edited text. In the earlier *enuma elish* he is a being who is male and female, one. (See Iraq statue matching this description.) I propose that this androgynous spirit God is the atom, and a being, too. It match-es the Jewish star, which is their symbol and flag! I theorize that the first creation of man in Genesis, coincidently on the sixth day, is nature's creation/evolution of these sky beings/gods of primitive man and is good. (Again see Iraq statue/evidence.) They, like everything else in nature (universal god) are made of atoms.

The Bible continuously puts God "UP" in Heaven. They conquered space. It is always trans-lated from the Hebrew word meaning "sky." We are in it, and it is made of atoms, too! It clearly says Adam was created in his creator's image.

But are we the sixth day creation or the eighth. The eighth is the one where he is named Adam and mimics science. The sixth evolve and become chil-dren of the sun, like the Earth. It is made of atoms! The eighth day Adam is the FIRST "son of God," not the sixth. So this explains the father concept and the mother goddess as well. All cultures have sons and not daughters. (See evidence like the first man god of Egypt, Atum/Adam.) Coincidence?

I now know why this invisible god confusion exists and there aren't daughters in Heaven. The universe/sky/Heaven only creates/gives birth to sons/suns. (See Genesis project.) History does, too. There are no daughter of god rulers.

Wow, what a connection! I always wanted an answer for this religious story that excluded women in Heaven. Here's the point of reasoning for an actual physical god, besides "UP." Image is form, and it says we were made in His image. We have to look like him. This is logical, as my son looks like me. The earliest statues of god were big, bald-headed, big-eyed, frail-looking characters. (See Iraq statues and all alien-looking gods.)

What? How can this be? I thought he was "EVERYWHERE"? He is, and we are, atoms! We are stardust. But we can only make sense of this confusion by considering the mixing of these alien-looking gods and knowing physical science. However, solving our mystery is as simple as tracing the gold connection. It will solve what they look like and where they come from. Remember, our purpose is to work for them, and gold is their desired product. This purpose is the reason they purposefully stay away. Read on!

Gold is our ancient and current unifying force in the economy. It was and still is associated conveniently with God! This ancient religious convenience MATCHES today's science, because gold is now important for space travel. If only Heaven were replaced with space, it would all become so clear. Erich Von Daniken says this, too. (See evidence.) History/time must've progressed until this little alien/god obviously couldn't control his "sons." The halo soon followed when man made himself god. (It is exactly what happened. See Babylonian symbol for god.) This became the logical symbol used to tell man from god. It matched their craft! (See cave drawing on front cover.)

This same religious evidence is universal. (Gods first, then Sons, last kings began thirty-five hundred years ago.) And "COINCIDENTALLY" enough now, the majority of the religious world is waiting on a Jewish man named "Jesus" to return and save us from ourselves! His title included God, son of god, king, and ultimately MAN! He became the most famous man on Earth two thousand years ago by predicting his death and resurrection (rising from the dead). His fame and death was a result of "PERFECT TIMING" in place and history, which gave him irrefutable world-wide fame. "AGAIN, COINCI-

DENTALLY," the Jews are the most famous people on Earth and "dominate our historical timeline" and, unfortunately, scientific ones as well. (See gold chart.) However, some of us scientists see the evidence of our past. We have much older gold artifacts. (See all gold art evidence.) TRUTH/EVIDENCE speaks for itself, no matter what religious men say. (See quotes on last page.)

Now back to Jesus: He professed to be an immaculate conception (conceived from a virgin and god, even this implicates us as an evil creation) and achieved this because "A STAR LED" three wise men (priests) to kill him. They were told of him "IN THEIR DREAMS!" (Aborigines have dream communication, also. Heck, it's in every religion! However, the aborigines have the abduction phenomenon and the evidence! (See pictures.)

But, instead of killing him, they "miraculously" changed their minds along the way. Ironically, they helped make him the most famous man today, still. But is this really a coincidence, or is it predestined? He says it's destiny, like all religions do. We do have an alien abduction phenomenon. And if this isn't enough, he left on the clouds and said that he would return this way. Most importantly, he even said we came from "UP," and those who are worthy are going back "UP" with him! Wow, worthy! It must be about knowledge, because he called himself the word.

He told us to "FIRST SEEK THE KINGDOM OF HEAVEN/SKY/SPACE!" "Space is the final frontier," and the evidence is perfectly clear that the universe has already been conquered. At this point, I want to personally thank Captain Kirk/William Shatner for his "profoundly" famous quote that has been forever etched in my mind. Like Johnny Cash's encounter (see front cover of this book), Yeshua and the three wise men, and the famous painter from Italy four hundred years ago (also see front cover), he is another famous person to have this same experience. He had an encounter! There are many more, including President Jimmy Carter. President Reagan even prepared us for this possibility. Religion just over-shadowed it.

Oddly enough, I have always thought that I came from space; I mean the future. I know we're in space now. I have often envisioned myself in a much more technologically advanced existence.

One where we live in spaceships and not on Earth. They are the Hells of the universe and fit the down description. Lord knows, the news confirms this reality every day! Many times, I dreamed of being an astronaut. I even recognized this possibility in the Bible, with a quote by Yeshua/"Jesus." Obviously science and religion agree that it's already happened. He said, "Heaven is his throne and the Earth is a footstool." If Heaven is space, and the evidence seems clear that it is, then it has! When are we going to start addressing the religious story scientifically? If we do, the reason for our separation will make perfect sense! Thankfully, I have come to know that I am living in Heaven now. Even with all the Hell of mankind that surrounds me. Earth is a living paradise/Heaven/spaceship; only man makes it a dying Hell.

Buckminster Fuller said the same thing fifty years ago. He wanted to equalize wealth and was a great inventor/scientist! Otherwise, it is a paradise. Could the biblical story of man's being driven out of paradise be Mars? It is the sixth planet from the tenth, and man's biblical creation is on the sixth day. Could it have been another Earth? The evidence supports this possibility, like religion's destiny and déjà vu! They indicate that we are repeating history. It is the closest planet to Earth that will sustain life in the future of our ecosphere. (See Sumerian Mars tablet.)

Maybe everything is "living," even though we think it's not because it's man-made. Everything that exists now is nature's creation in the beginning, even what we create out of it. But not living like in "our" sense. Our sense is selfish. We did have proof of this with Roswell, New Mexico, in 1947. It was a flying saucer crash, which was alleged to be an organic type of spacecraft. We are currently working on this technology today, artificial "LIVING" material.

We are also working on "planet moving" to accommodate Earth for the inevitable expansion of the son/sun. It will have catastrophic effects for humans as a result of global warming. We know this is possible through the slingshot effect, which we now use for launching satellites. This works by a planet's gravity capturing the satellite and then slinging it into further orbit. We know the Earth could be pulled further out with a large asteroid. This would take an orbit of six thousand years. NO WAY! This is the Jewish calendar. It is also close to the seven thousand year orbit of the tenth planet.

Is this the reason we are a mystery, according to Bode's law? (Law of how planets form, and Earth shouldn't be here. It should be between Mars and Jupiter. There is an asteroid belt there. Just another example of today's science catching up with ancient religion!) Remember, this book is all about the Jewish millennium of peace being ushered in by contact. It's about the future. This possibility would fulfill their calendar of seven thousand years. Our six thousand years and the next one makes seven. COINCIDENCE? Well, if you think so, then you better check out the evidence of a tenth planet in our solar system. (See cave example with a rocket and asteroid belt between Mars and Jupiter; also Sumerian tablet pictures of Mars with nuclear symbol and flying saucer! All of these are in Sumerian tenth planet story as well as moon mystery!) It was known by early man six thousand years ago and has an orbit of seven thousand years. There's only one way this could be. Their god is a space traveler, and the tenth planet must exist. It does! Science confirms it and calls it Sedna.

Will the next thousand years confirm the scientific reality that I have discovered and just laid out? And again, most importantly, science has now confirmed its existence, and it is coming back! This can't be a coincidence. It's almost thirty-five hundred years ago to the day that kings started ruling! Even this evidence confirms its existence. Their first man god, Adam, started ruling twenty-five hundred years before that. If we accept this evidence, the millennium of peace rounds out the tenth planet orbit of seven thousand two hundred years! Are we on the verge of facing this scientific reality? Will it provide us with the slingshot effect? We are warming up! All these pieces of evidence are pertinent today. Does it support the alien/flying saucer phenomenon and explain religion's predestined mystery as well as modern man's? If so, now we know who came from up, why they created us, and, most importantly, what their gold halo means. We would all finally know gold's true value! This is all scientifically verifiable and MATCHES!

As for religious people who just believe their traditional religious leaders' answers, compare this evidence to your biblical story. If you have the halo and don't know what it means, please seek the answer or admit you don't know. But please stop saying you're "RIGHT!" This is self-righteousness, and Yeshua talked against it. Please "BELIEVE" the evidence only. (See Plato's quote and others.) This is why I have titled my last book in this research "2012: GOLD'S HISTORY SOLVES MANKIND'S MYSTERY!" It and the halo solve our mystery.

I love the Jewish quote, "Heaven's streets are paved with gold," because it makes scientific sense of religion's beginnings. All that we have to do is transpose religious terminology with scientific words. "Space planets are explored with gold!" It confirms today's reality of space exploration and our need for gold in doing so. I can tell you that my family and many other religious people don't know about the halo. And they probably won't seek. They don't seek, because they are convinced that their traditional religion is right. Their world has become the universal world of god/angels, spirits, and magic. They don't seek scientific knowledge! They won't consider this evidence, even though it comes from their "SACRED" Jerusalem, Israel, area. Moreover, the tenth planet evidence was given to us by the Jews (Sumerian priest) six thousand years ago. It was kept in museums, not to mention that it is now corroborated by science and a cave sculpture. This cave sculpture reflects an accurate knowledge of these facts that literally couldn't have been known by primitive man. It even shows a rocket between Earth and Mars, the asteroid belt, and the planets in their right size and distance from the sun. Most importantly, it shows space gridded. This is obvious proof they know matter in space is flat. It is today's membrane theory and infinite understanding of matter and the universe. (Again, see pictures.)

My last story climaxed with the "BELIEVING" part of all religions. It's obvious that our mystery/separation and eventual contact is all about this "UN-FOLDING" evidence. (Biblical quote: "When knowledge increaseth all over the Earth, Michael will do battle with its kings and the truth will prevail.") Am I this Michael and the truth this evidence? I don't know. But the evidence is incredible! I do believe the evidence will overwhelmingly prove that the alien is primitive man's god! It matches! This is the way we convict criminals, with matching fingerprints and DNA! Will my family believe that I am the Michael of their Bible story? I don't know. But I do know that they don't want to be an alien. I do think that my brother Brian is already accepting this evidence for what it is. It is what primitive man saw! Up is in every religion, and we have ancient art of flying saucers. The evidence says they exist. It's all there to see, that science has already achieved creation, space travel, and conquering death itself. Not that we can't be killed, but we can be brought back. Even universal mummification points to this scientific reality, and it certainly rules out a spirit world. Why else would they want the body preserved? We are doing this today with the science of cryogenics! (See comparison of religion to science.)

Can't people see that their religious traditions create pride/unscientific stubbornness/close-mindedness/self-righteousness? And it's all based solely on handed-down stories that man could've embellished with magic. Well, it didn't matter what I shared with my family, because they remained followers of tradition. Except for Brian; he became a "FACTS" man, "just the facts." I laughed and always thought about the two guys on "Dragnet." Two guys again; wow! Religious pride caused division or lack of logic, and if I pressed the issue, they would get mad.

How well I know that tradition causes people to get angry and kill over religion. Hell, the whole world knows. You don't talk about "POLITICS, RELIGION, OR HER!" I laughed out loud. Confronting the logic of these traditions is futile, and sex is the biggest cause of murder world-wide. There's nothing anyone can do about it. And that's okay. Believe me, I'm not afraid of them myself or anything else that exists. I am not even afraid of dying and not existing again! I am a scientist and know the law of matter/energy: It can't be created or destroyed. It is what it is, infinite. It is everything and it is US. We are stardust! (See alien sperm and face on shield.) This is religion's god-ISM and the invisible creator of the universe. It is the atom! The infinite creator of the unseen world. Matter itself is the issue. Is knowledge of it the most important thing to us? Does it really matter to us, or does what we look like "matter" the most? (These scientific word "coincidences" are kind of cool, huh?) I don't want to get old and ugly.

Well, I think I can say with absolute certainty that what we look like does matter. Our mystery exists, and beauty rules this planet, not science. It will be beautiful when science does. (See Plato, last page.) Again, I am a scientist and I believe in Yeshua/"Jesus." His teachings are all about knowledge, which is inner and forever. Outer beauty is powerful but only temporary, fading with time!

I hope you will enjoy my discovery that Yeshua is a scientist, too! He was a "time traveler" sent to teach quantum physics/religion (the atom/unseen world) to ignorant humans! He became frustrated at the magic world of his so-called religious leaders. His mustard seed parable about Heaven even proves that nature grows/evolves. Instantaneous magic doesn't exist. The mustard seed could be compared to the atom, which is in us/Adam, and makes up the entire universe. And when it "grows" we can live in its "branches" like the fowl of the air!

The sky is the best protection from evil man. Even this implicates our universal evil on Earth. We must become scientists of the unseen world, the atom. We must learn about it because we are it!

(Learn how we are creating objects with nanotechnology, using atoms. This will eliminate the need for bulk materials. We will be making something from nothing.) WOW!

Yeshua even called himself the first-born of the dead, which would have been Adam/Atom. Coincidence? He said anything is possible. Did he create the first Arabic human with the knowledge of DNA, and have to sacrifice himself because of it? The story of his children is the story of two brothers. The Garden of Eden story consists of two trees and the "snake." This obviously reflects DNA, as it looks just like the AMA symbol. (See evidence. Other scientists have wondered what the true meaning of universal snake and dragon symbols mean. The evidence makes it clear.)

Anyway, this is good scientific food for thought. You can see the pictures to support these theories. The stories of reincarnation and the Gnostic book of Thomas support this scenario. He asked Yeshua/ "Jesus" how many souls are always coming into this world. He said one more than is leaving! Obviously, he is the "ALPHA and the OMEGA"! The bottom line is that he rebelled against religious leaders. They are anti-science. They use scare tactics to get people to follow them. Religion is terrorism, and science is knowledge! My family story proves beyond a shadow of a doubt that religion keeps people from seeking Heaven/universe. Not only do they not seek; they don't think it's possible to know everything, including the knowledge of our origins. I do, with science! They are religious and believe in magic. I don't! I propose that we are a scientific world and their religion is really "sci"-ence (sky-ence), except for their obviously cruel magic god.

They just don't "see" it. It's because they don't "seek it." I was shown early in life, by my third grade teacher, how handed-down stories proved man's "un-natural" tendency to stretch the truth. This display of our "un-natural" thirst for attention excites ourselves and proves our evil/animalistic "nature." We are tortured by the primitive side we were created from. This gives us our strong sexual/animal ego.

The story changed totally from the first kid to the twentieth! This is religion's downfall. It's only gone through sixty men at one hundred years each! And it's really all about sexual power. (See Cernes

Giant.) Everyone knows it's always been a man's world. The "FALL" is the angel/alien scientific creation of us. Religion's god description is Omni-SCIENCE, which is all-knowing. Come on, religious people, wake up, please! Religion even has a universal scientific story of how the universe "BEGINS" with nothingness. Science has the Big Bang, which says it "STARTED" from nothing, a single atom! Could their invisible God, which is symbolized by the Jewish star, be the atom? They match! (See symbols.)

This explains how he creates Heaven and Earth, which is void and without form. (Two things again: the nucleus and its outer ring of electrons. See universal art depicting a circle with a dot in its center.) How, scientifically or religiously is Heaven/space "created"? (It is really full of fragmented atoms that don't have a beginning, and nothing is an oxymoron.) The symbol for infinity is a figure eight. Again two things: Heaven/space is ruled by chaos, and god/atom "MOVED"/spontaneous combustion(heat)/natural selection became the catalyst for order/life to begin. The atom must have a natural encoded knowledge to multiply.

The Egyptians say that out of this infinite chaos, which is nun/nothing, was "born" the first man-god named atum/adam/atom. He seeded the universe from himself through masturbation. Again, Big Bang, literally! The Jews say that the first man/son of God was created from the ground; his name also was Adam. Then Eve was created from him! (See Iraq statues, which are androgynous. Today we can clone!) Science says that we literally are born from this universe of chaotic, fragmented atoms, and we are atoms! We are literally sons of the sun. This is why there aren't any daughters in the universal sons of god story. God is the universe and just creates suns/sons. All gods including Yeshua called themselves the sun/morning star. Religion literally is universally rampant with the scientific empirical evidence of how galaxies are born from this "nothingness" (fragmented atoms) and evolve/change to create life through nature's process.

I propose this to be natural selection. Science explains this process through the Big Bang and explosion/fission of this energy/matter/nothingness, through time. And time really doesn't exist; when matter is infinite and connected it just changes form. Religion does this by saying death is like sleeping. I was always blown away with the sixth day creation story of the Jewish Bible. The Jewish star and atomic symbol match and are six-pointed geometrical figures. They are both also a universal symbol! They describe the same scientific creation/evolutionary process of galaxies/solar systems/planets by nature. This is called natural selection, and all life is a creation of nature or its "crea-tures!"

Even mankind is nature's creation, only through un-natural means. We're like ligers or plastic. We wouldn't exist through natural selection or evolution. We must be a scientific creation. I believe that we "can" know it all through science, even what religion's god looks like. This is obviously the $64,000 question. Why else would they stay away? Our mystery literally exists because no one can make them show up. Obviously, it exists this way, so anybody can refute the archaeological evidence by primitive man. It's the only way that this god's will/destiny/plan can and will continue.

Our separation and mystery is infinite! And for this reason, believing is how the story climaxes when they return. What is their plan? Gold's universal history and its current status make it obvious. It must be for us to continue worshipping/working for them. It's all about the gold, and if we don't want to be killed, then we better not challenge religion. But, I am questioning their story and challenging instant magic! I am ashamed of their killing god and can't see why they don't challenge it as well. It creates killers!

Even as I write this, I am still shedding a tear and reeling from the horrible pain, along with the shocking disbelief, at the recent headlines. It's happened again! But how could it? How could this happen again? This is the reason I challenge them, not because I think I'm Michael the arch-angel. This remains to be "SEEN!" I challenge them to help ease the suffering of those who are religious and lost a loved one due to a freak tragedy. I have to stop religion with this evidence, but then I realized it wouldn't stop brain-washed people. The headlines spelled this reality out for me. A mother cut off her eighteen-month-old daughter's arms because she had a dream that God told her to do this. He said she would go to Heaven, to be with him. Who would want to be with a killer?

If you think this is sick, then open your eyes and read the Bible. It provides proof of this horrible reality, a parent killing his/her child. Tragically it does, many times! I provided hard proof of this horrendous religious side effect in my last book. (See pictures on last pages of book.) It is a terrible disease that we can scientifically cure. But, we won't, according to their own story, and I tend to agree. It's predestined! But, I have to do this to "SAVE" as many children as I can. From religion!

Well, I said I don't see why they don't see this, but I do "SEE." I've opened my eyes and realized that following preachers who don't "see" this themselves is illogical. Yeshua/"Jesus" called us the blind following the blind. I used to be a follower. RELIGIOUS FOLLOWERS OF RELIGIOUS PREACHERS. But, now I questioned them and started researching/ "real seeking." I immediately quit thinking I was right and started researching other cultures/religions. They are all one and the same. I don't ever want to be right again. Religion and self-righteousness are also one and the same. It's all about the evidence. It will prevail. It doesn't lie; man does. I found that all civilizations/cultures/cities began with religion!

And Religion itself is still the best evidence that space is already conquered. The evidence is small, one word, two letters. The evidence will tell the "TRUTH" about our origins. All religious writings say "HEAVEN IS 'UP'!" I have put the timeline chart on the first page to prove this moment of mankind's mystery/"creation." It is the transition from primitive to "modern"/civilized man. It is when religion began. This chart plainly shows the evidence that led me to my theory. It will definitively and chronologically prove that this is all about the gold. It will reveal the sad reality that our scientific creation/ad-DIC-tion happens infinitely on every planet.

It's sad because WE ALWAYS HAVE TO BE SAVED! We always threaten Earth's destruction, with our egotistical, sexually driven, materialistic greed. I am guilty myself, and now I am seeking the answer to "MY" cure. I am ad-DIC-ted. Abstinence is the only key for the end of my insatiable appetite. I welcome their return. I started looking at other cultures. I discovered that the Mayans have the most accurate calendar of all cultures/religions. The ending date matches a projected declining pattern in the Earth's algo-rhythms (magnetic fields that are life-supporting systems).

Could this be the Earth's death? The religious stories say so. Contact is just the beginning of the known end to an old Earth. But a new one will arrive. Could this be the tenth planet or Mars? Read on! This "second-coming" date adds up to 12, 12-22-2012 (like the ten planets, sun, and moon), and it sounds like "My-end." But it's not the end of the world, just the end of time. It's the beginning AGAIN! A beginning where we are together again with the ANGELS/ALIENS/GODS, because they have to save the Earth from us. (This is only temporary: one thousand years.) Could it break in half, and produce gold everywhere? (We recently saw this reported in all newspapers. Asteroids are full of gold!) Wow! Mars could have its catalyst for an atmosphere, too: explosions. Could this be my ending story? Read on!

According to the Mayans, they will usher in the "GOLDEN" age. Coincidence? All religions call man's creation the GOLDEN age. Coincidence? In the beginning we were together and were perfect. All religions have a "second coming" to save the

Earth. Aren't we obviously just doing this again? But, why not just let our species exterminate itself, if we are such a bad thing? Doesn't this prove that we can't stop existing, like matter and energy's definition says so?

And image is obviously what this mystery is all about. I propose that our creation and mystery is a lust for sexual power. We can build robots! They wouldn't have done it if it wasn't for this. The golden age story and its demise proves it. We became materialistic. Every religion states that this is the cause of our separation. This is obviously why the golden age came to an end. Atlantis tells how we became materialistic for power. Are we finally about to find out why we can't co-exist with each other? Can we stop existing? And could this truth about ourselves be "UGLY"?

Nature selects only "ONE" way, and that is to multiply. Everything has only one root origin, like the universe itself. Natural selection makes sense for the good of its own existence, Wow! I will address the other two views about the universe and its origin later. They are creation and evolution. Could they really all be one and the same, like religion's trinity, if it wasn't for the instant magic of creation? Believe me, they all exist. We create and the world evolves/changes. Nature does select as shown by Darwin and the Galapagos Islands and other places with unique life. Now again, please, for our children's sake, let's solve this mystery because it's about "TIME"!

These Heavenly beings don't have it, and our separation/mystery is because one-third of them lusted for power. (See evidence of Sanskrit war in Heaven, just like Jews: one-third!) We have it as well as time! However, time is relative if we start pushing nuclear buttons! It is a dangerous, threatening global dilemma. That's what's mind-blowing about my name being prophesied to battle with the kings of the Earth. They control the buttons! I matched the Jewish Star to the nuclear symbol! wow! Unbelievable, huh?

Well, this mystery of us and them is what I propose to solve! Power comes from looks! Could we be aliens, addicted to beauty of the flesh, and could we have done this before? The archaeological/scientific evidence says so, and religion does too! "There is nothing new under the sun," "all is vanity," and "man is evil" are all quotations from the Bible. They support this possibility. Science does as well with the drake equation. And we know why they don't show. Could we be them?

In religion, we started with one language, and it says we will end with one. It's obviously English, and in the brain it's digital. Mathematics is the perfect language of the universe. For this reason, I will now tell you that the most famous man had his name falsely changed from Yeshua to "Jesus." This is why I have been putting "Jesus" in quotation marks. The Bible even says we will be hated for his name's sake. I theorize that his name gives us our answer.

He said that we came from up and must return as equals. We can only be equal through looks. The evidence shows one alien was present with primitive man. Could we be them, and addicted to the scientific creation of modern man's powerful beauty? I have déjà vu and am sexually addicted to outward human beauty, especially that smallest and most valuable piece of real estate in the universe. It's only six by nine inches in size and is what gives us all our immediate power over one another. My scientific observation of mankind is that we are all addicted to beauty and have déjà vu.

The most famous man on Earth is named YESHUA! Could we be these aliens addicted to our own scientific creation, which is all about power through beauty of the flesh? Remember the Old Testament name I am? Well, if his name is important for solving our mystery, then I AM and YESHUA! We all have déjà vu, and religion teaches reincarnation! I would like to dedicate my research to him also, and as I said before, my precious mother. She is the most "LOVING/BEAUTIFUL" parent any child could possibly ask for. She gave her life for us and was never vain. She kept me from fear, pain, and terror. She is LOVE with a capital L. Dad is the luckiest man on Earth. He got everything I wanted, the most beautiful woman in the world (inside and out), a beautiful family, and the little white picket fence. It's just a shame he couldn't control his ego and always be a humble person. For the times he was, I thank him and will forever be grateful. Humility is the greatest achievement we can reach.

REACH HIGH, UP TO THE SKY, FOR YOU TOO CAN REAP MY MILLION DOLLAR PRIZE. (The answer is in the third book. My hint goes to Nikola Tesla, who wanted to give the world free utilities/electricity.) I would also like to thank my friend Billy for his friendship and laughing at my six-by-nine real estate thing. He knows what I mean, and I'm glad my humor could help heal his heartbreak. Thanks so much, Dwayne Sheffield, for discovering religion is science before me. (Well, except for the obvious like magic and god killing his children. Oh, yeah, and not making the world perfect if he could.) Your book is a great contribution to humanity. And I don't think it's a coincidence we have the same title, "THE TWO WITNESSES and the. . . ." (Just type in his name on the Internet to get his book.)

And don't worry, I'm not getting above my raising, as Lester and Earl would say. This is my wife's famous grandfather, of the duo FLATT and SCRUGGS, who did "The Ballad of Jed Clampett." Without Lester's royalties I couldn't have done this. Thank you, Lester, Granny, and Tammy! Thank you so much! Dwayne, I now know life's about "reciprocity" (what comes around goes around or the third law of physics: "For every action there is an equal and opposite reaction"), not reciprococity. (Ha ha, my mispronunciation of it gave us all a laugh.)

So, please don't worry about me, I am thankful. My brother Brian said he thinks that maybe what I do best is laugh at my own mistakes. I'm laughing! And I'm sure that we are just doing what's already been done before. I'm sure it will be done again, and I'm definitely sure that I'm not the only one doing it now! Knowledge is omnipotent, always omni-present, and like my brother Brian will tell you, it is the most powerful thing in the universe. Of course, he knows it and love are one and the same.

Who would do something evil, knowing it will come back "AROUND" to bite you in the ass? You'd have to be a "STUPID-ASS"! Oh, by the way. Please take his advice and "don't assume anything; it makes an ASS out of U and ME!" He lets me know that sometimes I am one. I've looked a few gift horses in the mouth and come out on the wrong end. I think they call that a "horse's ass"!

Well, I don't mind telling you that I have, be-cause I'm lucky to still be here. Right, Dwayne! I thought I missed a few good opportunities until I met Dwayne and Joann. And then I really learned RECIPROCITY/DESTINY. Thanks again, Brian, you're the best. But, then again, you're all the best. I don't choose favorites. Ha ha ha. Thanks, Phillip, for being a great friend. What am I saying? To Hell with that. Me, you, and Dwayne, we are the 3-D brothers. Ha ha ha. We all have the name, Duane, only spelled differently. Don't worry, you will see Rosie again, just like I will see my little nephew Danny again. Johnny and June would be proud of the way you loved her and still do. His wife Rosie is June Cash's daughter, and the story of how we met is unbelievable. He bought my book at Books-a-Million, thinking it was Dwayne's. He did this because it had a strange new cover. Freaky, huh?

Well, we've all become the best of friends and even songwriters together. You are a great songwriter and she is a great singer! You're a match made in Heaven. Children are so special, and my nephew Danny sure is that to me! Shoot fire, I just want to thank all my family. They are a TREASURE, and they're all special! Family is what makes the world go round! Thanks again, Dwayne, Lyle, and Joann for all your help with my book-signing trips through Dallas. Your gift of music is truly something I will always cherish. You are great singers and songwriters, too! Lyle, you are a STAR! Hell, you're Waylon made over, and the world always needs another one like him. Thanks, buddy. I sure hope I haven't left anyone out, because I didn't mean to. I'm just brain-dead. Ha ha ha.

I WOULD GIVE MY LIFE TO SAVE CHILDREN FROM THE HELL THAT WE ADULTS PUT THEM THROUGH! Most of all, I wish I could give Danny back to my brother and his wife. He was killed in a tragic accident. I would make the world perfect if I could, because I know they would, too, but I can't! (The universe is filled with flying rocks!) But, I want you to know that I'm still a kid at heart and hope I always will be. So please forgive us adults, little children; we are sexually tortured. We think too much about ourselves. I hope we can scientifically improve upon ourselves. Therefore, with the following evidence, I am proposing a new theory about our origins to the world.

Theories have to be based on physical scientific evidence. This is all verifiable! I want to leave you with a quote by Erich Von Daniken: "We are at the threshold of a utopian year in which scientific evidence will solve our mystery." I have used some of his pictures from *Gold of the Gods*. They depict the aliens with the pyramids on gold tablets! We have no depictions in Egypt of man building the pyramids! This is why they remain a mystery, like the Easter Island heads, Nan Madol, and other huge structures that we still can't build! I hope Erich will seriously consider my theory. He wants to know what these "ancient astronauts" look like and why they don't contact us. His evidence is GOLDEN! It's from his book, *Gold of the Gods*! He supports the theory that the universe does the same thing anywhere life can exist. Einstein does, too! So does ancient writing on "GOLD" art. (See ancient Chinese art. It says anywhere the sun shines, life will exist!)

Author's final thoughts

THIS CONCLUDING story, like the previous three books, is a fiction based on real scientific discoveries and the actual historical/archaeological timeline of mankind. Some characters are authentic, while others were kept in their original fictitious status. I've done this in order to finalize and cohesively support the original storyline.

My previous trilogy of books chronicled this scientific research and story of my attempt to solve man's mystery. (See reviews.) As the title implies, I theorize that the following scientific/religious evidence will solve our mystery. I have discovered the infinite nature of energy and matter. Their definitions are the same and can be looked up in any dictionary. They can't be created or destroyed and come from "nothing" (fragmented atoms). Science would call this unseen "creator" the atom. Religion also calls it Adam/god, and we do create!

This is where my search began, in 1989, with religion. Why does modern man have such a short recorded history? This was the first logical evidence: that the universe was already conquered. Primitive man went for millions of years and never achieved knowledge to create anything. Why didn't we? Come on! We should have a longer history. Everything else natural does. We're just like plastic and TVs, recently created. Our short history is directly connected to our creation stories of primitive ancestors and his god.

This mysterious creation sparked an intelligence that quickly made us aware of ourselves and gave us the ability to recognize this mystery. It seems to have self-imposed an innate duty or desire to rediscover this creator. This knowledge grew out of scientific exploration. We are compelled by it to solve our mystery. I propose that science will finish the job, the same way it started, with science.

Religion just doesn't make sense. It creates many questions. They love us and yet stay away?

They're perfect, but made Hell and us? Why do the stay away and when did it start? All primitive cultures believe in creators from the sky who "created" them. Could this be a scientific coincidence, when they weren't global or scientists? This was the second piece of solid evidence that the universe could already be conquered by intelligent/"creative/scientific" beings. These are just two pieces of evidence that went into this book. There are many more, and they all add up to a tortuous conclusion for those addicted to the beauty of mankind.

I have put a lot of serious thought into this final book, which was supposed to be the last one on this subject matter. I did so because of our mortality and my/all fragile children. Death is a harsh reality. It's hard enough as an adult, but it's really hard as a child. So, I can imagine what a horrible moment this will be to a tender young adolescent like my son. I remember it well myself, and how my parents tried calming me.

Involuntarily, an emotional outburst erupted from me like a volcano. My body heaved from the unstoppable outpouring of convulsive crying. I cried rivers, and it was terrible. I don't think I've ever been more scared and cried so hard. I was much younger than my sons when it happened to me, because my parents were practicing Jehovah's Witnesses/Christians. When it did happen, I suddenly cried out with fright, and the tears started flying. My eyes got as big as dollars, and I ran out of my bedroom into theirs. I threw myself onto their bed and immediately went for my mother's safe, reassuring arms.

They didn't have to ask me what was wrong. I was already begging and pleading for them not to let me die, and to please tell me that I won't. They didn't have to ask me what it was that made me think this way. They knew that I had just seen grandpa die, and their religion made it painfully clear that we died. I never realized it before then.

Children don't think about death, or, at least, they shouldn't have to. It's too painful! My parents are religious. They couldn't explain my existence scientifically. And I was much too young to deal with death, anyway. I didn't understand the horrible fear that it caused me. However, they tried their best and explained their religion's viewpoint. Their religious answer was confusing, with the idea of two rewards, spirit in Heaven and flesh on Earth. If you didn't get the reward you were just non-existent. No! I couldn't stand the possibility of not existing, at least until I found out more from other religions. Wow, did I ever find out more. The other denominations believed in a burning Hell. This was much worse. Man, this couldn't be real! This was a nightmare. I wanted to know why their loving God didn't make the world perfect, and this was out of the question. Because they couldn't answer that.

I couldn't begin to understand where God came from, because they couldn't, either. They were religious! My parents never looked at religion through scientific eyes, and they wouldn't, because their religion mistrusted science. I even remember them letting children die from not accepting blood transfusions. Oh, God, no! I remember how this worried me a lot. They were anti-science about our origins and the universe's. (See anti-science JW evidence.) Their answers made my fears worse. Finally, my Mom just hugged me and said to not "think" about it. Wow! They planted this fear, and if I didn't think about it, I didn't have it.

I stopped. I finally grew up to be an educated scientist. I learned that their inability to answer these questions was a reflection of their religion and its own inability to answer them. It wasn't them. They were just religiously brain-washed but couldn't see it. In fact, they denied it even though they fit the symptoms. They saw that others could be, but not them: the classic symptoms of denial and blame. This was the problem I had to solve, the old "pot calling the kettle black" saying. Not only for my son, but for the world's children. I want them to know why religion's God didn't, and doesn't, make the world perfect.

But most importantly, where he came from, what he looks like, and why he stays away? And why he is a "HE," especially for the girls. I do this through science and am still overwhelmed by the simple evidence. It makes our origins, gods, and the universe self-explanatory. Just follow the evidence.

I conclude that religion is government-approved terrorism and harmful to children. I was terrified of it and still am as an adult, uncle, and father. This is a fact! And, for this reason, I have given this book the most serious attention I could. I thought long and hard about my final answer to our mystery. I mean to tell you that I gave it "all I had." This is what Yeshua wanted from the rich man!

Oh, what I would give for the beautiful possibility of being able to prevent children's pain. I would give my life, like Yeshua, to keep this from my sons and the children of the world. How can I prove our infinite existence to them and keep them from being afraid of death? I knew this wasn't possible, as things die, but please, always remember they never stop existing. I thought of Lester's song "Mother is only sleeping." Yeshua said this about Lazarus. I hoped so for Steve and Mary. I knew so. This is scientifically provable. They just change form. I know the evidence will prove our creation by "god/ aliens" from the sky. They, too, shared science's infinite nature. I am trying to discover how they conquered death. The religious story says so! Universal mummification points to this reality. Resurrecting cryogenicized DNA does too! I knew this was possible to solve, as anything is possible; well, except magic and preventing death.

This wasn't! It was an obvious, painful fact of life. But maybe, just maybe, they have the science to give it life again and preserve it forever. (See religious themes.) This is a beautiful thought, and science is making real progress with it. It even seems like a reality in our very near future. Therefore, I set out to do this for the children of the world. I did it so they wouldn't have a fear of death nor any doubt where they came from. But most of all, where they are going.

And in doing so, I owe my life to my sons. I owe it for having exposed them to the same realization of death at such an early age. I also was a product of my religious raising, but I have overcome my fear of death through science. I now know reciprocity, that for every action there is an equal and opposite reaction. If this is happening here, it is happening there, and it is happening everywhere.

This is the infinite nature of everything. I don't remember my first son's freaking out over death, and only recently do with my youngest. His mother had a tumor develop on her breast. I can't believe that I became angry at her inability to hide this fear from my son.

I left one night as a result of this, because I was

so angry. My son didn't want me to go, but I had to. We had a lot of problems that I couldn't deal with! I was so angry. I came back two hours later, very ashamed. I hurt my son deeply. I hurt him badly, over trying to keep him from being hurt. I regret this deeply! Now, I understood my dad. I was walking in his shoes and wasn't even half the man.

My son means everything to me. I wanted to make sure that my answer comforts him and leaves him without any doubt about our infinite existence! I owed him. Therefore, I asked my thirteen-year-old son the simplest question I could. One that would give me an answer that I had hoped to achieve. An answer that clearly reflected the impact and simplicity of the evidence. It should speak for itself and to everyone old enough to understand science. He had to endure the most pain, from religious people's wrath and persecution of us. He lived it with me.

My other son was grown and gone when I started book-signing four years ago. I asked him, "Where are we going in the future, son, scientifically?" He replied excitedly, "Wow, Dad! We are going Up just like them, huh?" Wow, he got it!

"Yeah, son," I said with a big smile on my face. "Captain Kirk is right; space is the final frontier. It's Yeshua's Heaven." I can't begin to express the feeling I had at that moment. It was a warm, deep satisfaction that spread all over my body. I was actually trembling with excitement as well. I literally felt a tingling sensation on my scalp, and it raised the hair on the back of my neck. I had done what I had set out to do. It was the greatest gift that I felt I could give to my sons.

Suddenly, I thought about probing his mind further, but he confirmed my nagging suspicion. He did this before I could get a chance to ask him the next obvious question. "Man, Dad, this means we could have done this before." He instantly slapped himself.

"Why did you do that?" I quickly blurted out in complete surprise.

"What?!" Angel remarked.

"Why did he slap himself like that?" I asked with a gruffly demanding voice. "That's crazy!"

They both just looked at each other as if I were crazy.

"What?" I asked again, not understanding

their weird behavior.

Then they both instantly replied, "I've . . . he's always done that."

"What?" I asked quickly. "Déjà vu?"

"Yeah," he replied cocking his head to the side, giving me a big-eyed look. "You didn't get it. I've always had déjà vu and never understood it till now. Maybe I have done this before."

"Yeah," Angel remarked with a laugh. "He does it all the time."

"Wow, Matt, and what do you mean by maybe?"

He just gave me that weird look again, like he knew we did. He read my mind and knew I was reading his. He knew that I had just spent the past ten years of my life trying to figure this out. I always knew it was the best proof that we could be from a "future" scientific reality, déjà vu itself.

Religion's universal teaching of destiny points to this fact! There is no other explanation for this, and the evidence is everywhere. We have existed before and will again. Science and religion both agree. If I could only get them to see man's scientific SEXUAL flaw. Outward Beauty is religion's "FALL" story and "EVIL." I knew this, all too well. But getting them to see us scientifically was the hardest job yet.

The only "GOOD" thing about our beauty is the competitive nature it creates. And that's good for their purpose and our destiny. I thought about religion's free-will. It sickened me! Mankind is destined and it's all about the gold. We aren't a good thing, and we better save ourselves. I hope they will see this because I can't make them. I can't make anybody. That's why the millennium of peace is just a millennium. I can't cure mankind!

I immediately hugged them both and couldn't believe what was happening. Instead of cringing as usual, my son joined in. It was a beautiful family moment, a real Kodak moment in space and time!

Here are the simple facts about our species: We have a SHORT HISTORY rooted in "GOLD"; pyramids and mummification everywhere; no open extra-terrestrial contact; RELIGION universally saying we were created to worship/WORK for them; ancient art of science symbols and spacecraft showing gold halo protection; a world-wide alien phenomenon that supports an existing futuristic science; ancient head molding; ancient art of god with a big head and halo everywhere; currently creating new life-forms and recreating ourselves; currently working on teleportation and anti-gravity, cloaking devices, holograms, conquering space, nanotechnology; creation with the atom, eliminating need for materials; growing organs for transplantation; cybernetic decoding of RNA with gold atoms; and finally ancient "TREPANATION"! Scientists currently theorize the ancients were doing "BRAIN SURGERY."

I theorize they were doing brain enhancement for the purpose of telepathic communication with their representatives/kings. We haven't found X-ray machines; only the elite were getting this done, and we now have successfully achieved mental abilities through cybernetics directly on the brain. The skull had been the inhibitor of our success with skull-caps. We have overcome this obstacle with trepanation.

The ancient were using GOLD tools! All this science mirrors ancient religious themes. We need gold for space travel! The most abundant rock to find gold is in quartz! They built pyramids for the workforce to see what to look for. And no wonder it was the temple for the gods of the SKY! Just think about what advances we will achieve in the next hundred years, let alone one thousand! It's easy to image that the pinnacle of science will and has been reached already. BRAIN-TRANSPLANTATION!

This would certainly explain déjà vu! We have just discovered that the brain alone (outside of the skull) is the immediate cure for our g-force problem of space travel! wow! wow! wow! We have and are about to, again, read each other's minds. The little voice in our head can be electronically deciphered into digital sound and imagery! This is the universal language. It will happen when contact and the millennium of peace begins.

I just watched the Science Channel and discovered another amazing piece of evidence. Well, two, actually. We just landed on Saturn's moon Europa with a probe, and it was so cool. It brought home my point about "UP" and the gold thing. The probe is mostly gold, like all spacecraft! Again, science is catching up with the ancient religious teaching of "UP"! The Genesis Project not only explains gold's purpose, but also diamond's, ruby's, sapphire's, emerald's, jade's purposes. They were the plates that captured atoms from the sun! Shocking, huh? This explains their religious depiction with the gold crown of god and its jewels! (Again, see comparison chart of science to religion.)

But most important is ancient religion's practice of trepanation. Today's science explains why it was being done by the ancients. We are now able to telepathically control the computer with electrodes. They are implanted directly on the brain "beneath the skull"! Religious ancient trepanation now also comes full circle, like up, gold, and "CREATION!"

Human bodies and robots are the most expensive commodities on Earth. Slavery is ancient. In Heaven, they read each other's minds, and we are again on the threshold of the same! Now I know why this answer was always in the "BACK OF MY MIND!" But will we want to? Since this mystery exists now, it's obvious some won't and it will always exist! (See war in heaven evidence.)

I hope I can do it. No, I will do it, for HOPE's sake. (My little cousin, I love you and look forward to seeing you again. It's been thirty years!) I want to leave you with a quote from the book of James. (James is a fraudulent name and not the correct

Jewish name of its Hebrew writer Yacob/"Jacob.")
"He/god hath reserved chains of darkness [Earth
and gravity] forever, for these angels [aliens] which
kept not their first estate [body], but left it for a
strange flesh [mankind] and return like a dog to
vomit [reincarnation]."

Could we be them? I am! Yeshua! December
22, 2012; the struggle continues. This is the Indians' great purification. The beginning "AGAIN" of
the Mayan golden age. And the final "JUDGMENT
DAY" of the Jewish people. The millennium of
Peace begins with the angels'/aliens' return! We are
not this body. We are aliens! Will we see mankind
for what we are scientifically? An inevitably self-destructive nuclear evil. If so, WWYD? Welcome BACK
to our SCIENTIFIC FUTURE! It is all happening again,
now.

Conclusion: "Judgment Day." 12-22-2012. The millennium of peace begins!

12-21-2012! That time is now. I can't believe this is happening. The Jewish "Judgment Day," the Hopi's great purification, and the one I found to be the most accurate, the return of the Mayan "Golden Age." But I have to admit the Hopis hit the nail on the head. It is a purification process all right, and we are the mess. "We are judged already." This is written in red! We are dead now. We Die! Tomorrow, 12-22-2012, we start the clean-up! We live! We live for tomorrow, the future. That's science.

I thought long and hard about my first world-wide appearance, well, the third, upon my return to Nashville. At least, I wouldn't get shot out or killed in this one. I knew we were judged already, from my research. Our "pre-ordained" judgment was something that Yeshua said to the Jewish preachers constantly, and it's obvious because we are alone. Yet, they didn't get it. He clearly told us that only those in heaven were good.

I can somewhat understand the confusion of this simple observation because of their religion. But I didn't understand it today. How can this exist in a scientific world? We are a flawed scientific creation, and our religious creators knew it from the get-go. So the answer to our unfolding mystery has to lie in our purpose. They do stay away on purpose. Therefore, we must "SERVE" a purpose or can't be stopped scientifically. This is logic. It isn't logical if we are a "GOOD" thing. I found both to be the case. We are addicted to outward beauty and this scientific creation possibility is becoming more obvious every day.

Our purpose is to worship them, and gold is their offering. Our creation makes all the sense in the world now, because nobody likes hard work and gold is in never-ending demand for space travel, medicine, and technology. Our species can outperform robots, ten to one. And our abilities really "SHINE" when you throw in the sexual power thing. The sky's the limit and it's limitless. But we aren't!

I watched as the sky was made brilliant by the blast of a nuclear bomb. Unfortunately, this is how we "SHINE," and yet the world religions call us a "Marvelous" creation. I watched in horror at the sight of my own death. I was watching the blast that took Jerusalem out and did me in. Or so they thought. I trembled in fear at the thought of continuing this infinite struggle. How could I change mankind's mind about our species?

We are so destructive, so viciously mean to each other. We are the most selfish beings in the universe, and we can't be stopped. Science is everywhere, "omni-present." But it is also what provides a safe "Haven/heaven" for those whose seek it. This is why we need the gold for heaven/space!

My desire to solve our mystery spawned a research into religion and ultimately finding the mystery. I am thankful to religion for this and its teachings of humility and anti-wealth. But the mystery became the most important teaching of all. It gave me anger control and stopped the "little voice" from ruining my life.

The mystery is the act that will OPEN your mind to the science of life and mankind's harsh reality. It is the catalyst for self-awareness and acceptance of boredom. In fact, it will make you crave boredom. Because when you're not doing it, you're acutely aware of the "HELL" around you. I knew I couldn't change anyone or anything. This was the most frustrating thing of all to accept. But, then I laughed to myself. I knew this from the first time I entered drug rehab. It was the serenity prayer.

We can't change anyone. I can only change myself. It was time to change my appearance. It was time to become "one of us," and we are one. I laughed at this because it was one of Jake and my first songs. "My Little Cowgirl" was first, and then it was next. This was life. Art did imitate life. Throw a beautiful women into the mix and it happens every time!

"Just kidding," as my uncle Brice would say. It was a shame how Eve is blamed from the get-go.

The religious world is so cruel to women. I didn't want to start thinking about this again. I needed to "lighten" up. Wow lighten up! Did I just say that?

I laughed again. Could I be an alien? I was so addicted to beauty. Then I quit laughing as I saw my death. I instantly saw the horror in my son's eyes. They saw the whole event on television. It was playing everywhere. The fate of the world was at hand, or at least as we knew it. It was about to be saved by our "glorified" brothers, the "ELECT"! They were pre-elected! There is nothing new under the sun. I suddenly thought about the sun. Would it still shine, in lieu of the ominous clouds of radiation that had to exist? I knew that the U.S. had been nuked just like Jerusalem. I knew the world had experienced partial global destruction. Seeing is believing with mankind! It would have kept going, but it was stopped at the critical point of no return. The aliens stopped it. But would they believe us now? Even if I make my debut as an alien.

Again, I quickly remembered the key to this mystery. DESTINY! Of course the majority won't. Even in the face of becoming a real-life alien nation. I loved that show and was always blown away by my lack of awareness of it. But then again, I realized that without magic our species and awareness of itself takes time. It multiplies!

This is life from the smallest level to the big picture. Science and the Bible are based on this principle. Multiplication! Like this second coming, it will only happen when knowledge increaseth all over the Earth, and we are threatening the Earth itself! This blew me away, still.

How could I not be this biblical Michael? How could Jake and I not be the two witnesses? He is religious and believes in spirits. I am scientific and believe in aliens. Wow, this is mind-boggling! Anyway, in the show, they were people with big bald-heads! The ancient alien evidence was being portrayed in hollywood all along. The most famous was E.T. He looked just like the Sumerian statues and owl man. Hell, even *Twilight Zone* had created a show where the E.T.s were ugly and all looked the same. The whole world was showing bits and pieces of the big picture, but only I had put this torturous puzzle together. This was so bizarre. It was déjà vu all over again. We have done this before and will do it again. This was what I had to never forget. We are judged already!

The sun was shining, but not for long. Sirens were going off everywhere. The entire U.S. was under a nuclear radiation alert. It was just a matter of time before it would affect us all. It already had. The world was in complete panic. The news showed the chaos taking place all over the world. My reception in Nashville was the same as Jerusalem. Except for the bomb. We were in control now. I wouldn't be killed again. I have the world's attention and am giving people the supposed "ultimatum." Actually, it was just time to finish the job and start all over again. We are aliens addicted to the scientific creation of mankind's outward beauty. We served our purpose as long as we could here. We would have annihilated ourselves.

I watched as Johnny and June were reunited with their family. Needless to say, it was awkward. But what could you expect? They were aliens. The family resisted until they touched the ship. It disappeared only to reveal their bodies. Everyone gasped in complete surprise. There bodies were laid out on two gurneys. They took them onto the spacecraft to view their bodies, which lay in suspended animation. It finally sank in as my friend Duane broke down and sobbed uncontrollably. He was going to see Rosie again. I was so happy for him.

Suddenly, the world understood universal religious mummification practices. They were seeing religion's story literally played out scientifically before their very eyes. The idea of another planet's being thousands, if not, millions of years scientifically advanced beyond ours was blatantly staring them in the face. Instantly, my theories of creating bodies any way that we want came to fruition. My job would be simpler now, but not easier. The Earth was full of people who didn't care about anything but themselves. This was, sadly enough, infinite!

I immediately went to Duane and thanked him for helping me. His family had resisted until this moment. Some still were. Some were leaving; no, not some, most. Would this happen to me as well? I knew better than to think any differently. Duane was trying to stop them, but couldn't. I held him back as he fought to make them stay. It was no use. But, then I showed him Rosie. She was in another craft accompanying ours. They were everywhere.

He ran to her and I followed. I knew this would be hard for him. That's my point. It's hard for us all to understand. We are so primitive in our scientific thinking and certainly are with our current level of technology.

I had to resist wanting to see everyone that had passed on. They were all here somewhere on these ships. This was the hardest thing that I ever had to do. Or at least I thought so. I was wrong. The hardest was to come, and it was starting already. My own family was beginning to crack. I saw them get out of a heavily guarded van. Little Jake was being carried by my oldest. They began to run toward me. Jake was screaming at the top of his lungs. I told them, Dad! I did, I did! You are MICHAEL! I hesitated as I turned from Duane and started toward them.

He quickly nudged me on. I'll never forget the look in his eyes as he did so. We loved each other unconditionally and were completely at peace with ourselves. He said to me softly as he wiped away the tears, "Go on, buddy you deserve it."

"We all do," I said, choking back the tears. "Especially Dwayne and Joann."

"Yeah," he replied quickly. I had to hug him

again before I left. I turned and ran to my two boys. I was squalling with every step I took. I couldn't stop thinking about Dwayne and Joann. I was overjoyed at the prospect of them seeing their son again. I thought about my brother David and his children. They will see him, too. I thought about Mom and my little sister Nancy. I was thinking about everyone! I thought about my brother Steve. He will get to see Danny!

I was overcome with joy as I finally reached my sons. We embraced for what seemed like an eternity. It wasn't long enough. I was about to have my own family breakdown, like he just did. My wife and her family soon caught up to us. I could tell by the look on their faces that they had mixed emotions. Especially her mother. She had been with me at the beginning of my journey. She had witnessed my name "MICHAEL" written on a bathroom mirror. She also read my books and watched these events unfold, just as I wrote them. She watched me do the mystery, become a vegetarian, and give endlessly.

But she nor my wife would ever do mystery. She never gave up her material world. Giving to others never took precedent over everything else.

My wife didn't either, nor anybody else. My family was no different. The whole world wasn't. And now our money and possessions were no good. The aliens could feed everyone. They had the technology. The only thing that was important now was giving in!

I reached and hugged them. I knew they would never make the first move. My wife started to cry uncontrollably. I stroked her hair and hugged her tighter. She started to apologize. I stopped her and told her I was sorry.

"I'm sorry for all of this," I said as I held her face and looked deeply into her eyes. "We've all made mistakes. Hell, I made plenty. I'm still making them. Here I'll show you. Give me a cigarette, Brenda."

She just laughed. I lit it, half-inhaled and threw it too the ground.

"See, I am equally ashamed of my past. Yes, even Michael Recycle is a fraud. I smoke and litter. What a joke, huh? I am not perfect. We all aren't, or we wouldn't be here. I know we should be, but it's all about the golden rule, not what we do to ourselves. Please, I'm begging you to be strong, for the kid's sake. There isn't any more time for us to think about ourselves. That's what our shame is. This body is the shame. It's time to get on with the 'PROGRAM'," I said lovingly with a southern drawl.

I was lovingly mocking her and Paul. He had influenced her so much. He was her mischievous, egotistical, materialistic step-dad. But in spite of this he had good intentions. He just liked being in charge of the "PROGRAM"! This was the shame of mankind. Our sexual organs tortured us with the "DESIRE" to be the "HEAD-DICK" in charge! We were cursed with the "NEED" to be worshipped, and ironically this was religion's purpose of a "loving god."

What a joke, huh? But hardly anyone saw this. No wonder his creation went to Hell in a hand-basket! His intentions were selfish and flawed. I laughed at the hand-basket saying. The biblical teachings and their influence in everyday conversation never ceased to amaze me.

I wanted to talk with them more, but was dangerously interrupted. Some of the angry crowd began to throw rocks. It was reminiscent of the biblical stoning. My body heaved and convulsed with disgust. I wouldn't let it get angry. I expected this from the "Religious" movement. Hell, they were even calling me the "Devil." This was "their" opportunity to make a statement in front of the world. Their "statement" was my "evidence."

My arrival alone had drawn a pretty good crowd. Not to mention Johnny Cash. I hurried the kids back into the van and sent them on their way. They wanted me to come. I couldn't, and little Jake knew why. I was so humbled by his strength. Jimmy's, too. They were my rock.

"Dad's got business to take care of," he said so boldly that it surprised me. He grabbed Angel's hand as he got into the van. She hesitated and then took hold of Jimmy's and climbed in behind little Jake. Brenda was the last. We looked at each other for a moment. That was all it took. She knew that I knew, and nothing else needed to be said. She was a proud woman. What a shame. I couldn't worry about that now. I couldn't change her or my wife. They are what they are. It's up to each of us to change ourselves, and actions always speak louder than words. The time was now and really is all we have if we want a better tomorrow!

This was my job. A better tomorrow. I had a thousand years of work ahead of me, and it was going to be a hard row to hoe. I was the Head-Dick in charge and still didn't know if I could control my own ad-DIC-tion to beauty. I was afraid to be myself.

I knew my real body was on the craft I just came from. What I didn't know was what I had to do next. How did I become it? I had to suddenly dodge a rock. What was I thinking? That was my cue. It almost hit me and the van. I hollered for the driver to go on. I knew what I had to do. I had to show the world I could allow this body to be killed, voluntarily. The world needed to see me do mystery as they pummeled me with rocks. This body is nothing but clay. My original body is the potter.

I turned to the cameras and sat down Indian style. I first addressed my children and told them what was going to happen. I told them it was time to put aside this body and make my ultimate sacrifice for their sake. Hell, for the world's sake. This was the beginning of mankind's end on this Earth. We were going to save it from them and leave only a few to start over again.

"Please don't let the kids see this, Angel," I said one last time before I began to do mystery. "This goes for all of you parents. It will happen quickly and it will be shockingly gruesome, but I will immediately be free. Then I will lead the charge to round up all those who resist the truth. There will be one final battle, and it will take place in the stronghold of religion. Megido Israel. This is their Armageddon."

I began to do mystery. The stoning was short-lived, and I was immediately back in my alien body. I still couldn't get used to the vertigo thing.

My body was nauseated at the aftermath. I knew what I had to do. I stepped out of the craft and was in complete shock at the sight of my bludgeoned, lifeless body. I went over to it. Not a soul threw a rock as I reached down and touched it. I turned to the cameras with tears rolling down my cheeks and said, "Forgive them father for they know not what they do."

I stood and told the world, "It is finished. I am glorified."

The body was immediately spontaneously combusted in a brilliant flash of light. They started to throw rocks again, but this time they were stopped. They were taken up into the craft by a beam of light. The ones who were watching started to run. I yelled out to them, "You can't run from yourself. Your time is short. You will all be recycled at the battle of Armageddon. It is already written."

I turned again to the camera and begged for my children and the children of the world to please not worry. "I will not let them hurt you or anyone else anymore. We will stop them. There will be no more violence and death until the Earth is cleansed from this disease called mankind and his 'religion.' We will do this with science and you will learn the wonders of it. You will no longer be afraid of death, because we have conquered it," I said.

"I will show you proof." I yelled for my deceased body to rise. The bludgeoned body came walking out of the craft and came to stand beside me. "This was done through science, and my departure is, too. I must leave now."

We both sat down and did mystery. I told them they would see me soon. We sat for a little while and suddenly we were gone in a flash of light.

I had returned to the craft and we departed in front of the crowd and world. They were still standing in complete astonishment at what just took place. They had seen the future! I couldn't wait to return to my children. I wanted to explain that this was science. There wasn't any magic, and this transition would take a thousand years. The Earth had sustained great damage and would get even worse. I knew they would have a lot of questions about aging and what was going to happen and when. I didn't worry about answering the world's questions. My books would do it for them. This was all about the gold and the restoration of the Earth. Tomorrow would bring a much better day for those who give. And for those who don't, the purifying begins.

We landed in the yard of a beautiful little cottage just outside Nashville. I didn't recognize the place, but quickly found out it was Nurse Gail's aunt's place. She had passed on years ago and left it to her brother. It was perfect. The kids quickly ran outside to meet me. After hugging the fire out of me, they wanted to see the inside of a real flying saucer. I could hardly believe it myself. I greeted them with the body they knew. I still didn't know how they would accept my having an alien body. Hell, I already saw how Johnny's family took it. Most didn't. Mine either.

I suddenly thought about Mom and Nurse Gail. Then I saw them come out of my craft. They were accompanied by our alien bodies, mine included. Wow, this was so cool. They must've been doing mystery to attain remembrance or religion's resurrection. I thought the kids would be afraid, but instead, they were pretty excited. I suddenly realized that Mom and Nurse Gail had been on the ship this whole time. They had been on there with Jake. I didn't have to ask where Jake was. I already knew. There was much work needed to be done to get Mars ready for this transition. It would be the next Earth. He was still resistant to his alien/glorified body, even though he did mystery.

We all went into the craft. I was still excited myself. The kids were awestruck. Then it happened. They wanted to see their bodies. I sat in the command seat and put my hand in the molded control box. I communicated with the other ships and had them beamed over. The bodies were in a state of animated suspension doing mystery. Little Jake surprised me by going over and sitting across from his. Jimmy quickly followed. They knew the mystery and began to do it. Mom and Nurse Gail just grinned real big.

I did too! I couldn't believe what was happening. I often wondered if they would do it when the time came. I made an impact. We joined them. This was a Kodak moment. We sat for awhile and nothing happened. Little Jake was getting fidgety just about the time Angel and her mother stepped into the craft. They screamed and Little Jake jumped up and ran to them. I got up and turned toward them.

"It's all right, Angel," I said softly. "Nothing's happening." Little did she know it was. But I couldn't explain this to either of them. I tried for the past twelve years. I wasn't successful with them or many of my family either. Nothing physical did happen when you do mystery, only mental. This was something that they were going to have to find out for themselves. But they had to get the courage to look at their real body first. "Yeah, Mom," Little Jake said as he consoled her. "Dad's right, nothing does happen. It's all right. Show her, Dad, get her and smoking granny's alien body here so they can see it."

That was it. Brenda high-tailed it out of there. Angel abruptly picked up Little Jake turned and followed her mother. She tried to act normally, but I knew this scared her. It was the first time seeing it in person. I didn't even need to ask where Granny Flatt was. I knew she would think this was of the devil. She wasn't about to come out here.

This was the reason it would take a thousand years to "purify" the Earth. It was also the reason cohabitation didn't work. It's the reason this mystery exists now. Some of us would never choose inner peace over outward Hell! Beauty of the flesh is what creates Hell.

We're all addicted to outward beauty. Will we return to our first body? This is my question to the world. WWYD?

I needed to have a good dinner and explain all this to my family. That question, for the entire Earth's population, will come tomorrow. But now I had to explain what the future held for us. It wasn't going to be pretty. Somehow, I always knew this would happen. I would have to tell the world what I already knew was inevitable. We would be able to read each other's minds tomorrow after I speak to the world. This technology and more would be revealed to the world. They would see our sexual downfall play out before their very eyes. We had all been implanted with chips that decoded our thoughts. I hadn't experienced a vision to know this. I just did.

It was the way the story of religion went. I also had to explain that there isn't any magic either. Transporting our population to Mars would take a long time—maybe even a thousand years. But most importantly, the world will see our technology. They will see how the religious story of creation is science. Most have already started to entertain this possibility with today's science or those who have read my books. They will finally see how stem cells can produce even brains with no memory. The idea of achieving immortality of memory is simple science. It will make reincarnation, déjà vu, and prophecy a reality. At least for most.

I often thought about the scripture, where Yeshua said, "You don't put new wine into an old wine sack" and the many references to mankind as "her." The references to the beings in heaven, with the father as one, became clear when I saw the alien and his overly large penis evidence. All the stories of them looking "DOWN" on the daughters of men and thinking they were pretty is "CRYSTAL" clear now, like quartz. But most of all, I need to explain to the world and my family why this exists. This is the ultimate cover-up in religion, besides "UP."

It's harder to "SEE" because Genesis makes man good. The up thing in heaven is irrefutable and we still don't "SEE" it. Even with today's space program and television telling us that up/space is our future. This is how you multiply and assure your immortality as a species. We have to overcome the stronghold of a "SINGLE" planet. We are at its mercy and are not technologically advanced enough to control it. I had to speak plainly about our need for mankind as a worker. The sexual nature that tortures him and impedes his better judgment also makes him viciously competitive and productive. Obviously our sexual nature (the aliens/angels/gods) did the same thing. Science gave this the ability to happen to us first and then them. Our creation became scientifically unstoppable in his pursuits.

I thought about the Tower of Babel story, and it was even clearer now than ever. This must've been the point of no return for mankind's creation. The oneness of his species in the beginning must've given him the ability to excel quickly. His competitive nature drove him to even attempt to get back to "HEAVEN"/SKY, where the real knowledge was, because that's where his came from. The separation from mixing with man, which was precipitated by the Flood, wasn't enough to stop him. He would continue in his relentless pursuit of Knowledge because it gave him scientific "POWER." It was the very thing that made his species. He is the most effective worker in the universe, but uncontrollable and an illusion. He would never exist if it wasn't for science, and his short recorded history, like plastic, has is the best proof. We don't question that science made it; it's only been around fifty years and most of us saw its creation.

But the majority of the religious world never entertains this possibility with us. This is unbelievable to me, when I repeatedly emphasize that religion's story of our creation is just like plastic. It was "CREATED" and has a short history. Hell, we are even creating new "LIVING" species today. We are seeing religion's story becoming a scientific reality right before our very eyes. My brother Brian made it very clear that I had to keep my explanation simple about why we exist anyway if were so destructive and they "KNEW THIS BEFORE-HAND, RELIGION'S DESTINY." This answer is simple. This answer is simple! It is in Genesis as well as every religion in the world: "God looked down and there was no man to till the ground.".There! That is our undeniable "TRUE" purpose. If I can just keep a religious person from trying to tell me that I can't know it all I'll do okay.

Brian watched me get upset at a few of them on occasion. They always take the approach that nobody knows the beginning of religion or the god word. Sadly enough, it was usually a young turk full of testosterone saying this to me. And he was usually a little too aggressive when he did it. How dare him to tell me that I can't know it all? That's my goal and I am achieving it through the Internet and science, history, biology, quantum physics, and finally what I really want to know, NEUROSURGERY! I would always ask them the date of religion's origin and they hardly ever knew. It was bad enough that they didn't know it and were teachers of it, but then they would tell me BLIND FAITH was enough for them. I usually got a little upset at this point, and Brian finally got to witness it. Even the pursuit of knowledge can be self-destructive in a world of "BLIND FAITH."

Why did I care anyway? This was why I wanted to be a brain surgeon. I wanted to "KNOW" the workings of the mind, thought itself. How could it become protective of itself like a living being? Of course, I already knew ignorance is bliss, but to really "KNOW" how neurons work. WOW! Neurons are the problem. You have to "NEUTRALIZE" them to prevent awareness of the self! If you don't, thought itself is self-destructive. It creates selfishness or self-righteousness. Even science can fall prey to it. That's why I always say I could be wrong; let the evidence speak for itself. We know when the god word began! But most of all we know where it came from: "UP"/heaven, and that is where we are going.

I went on in and had dinner. I thought about the scriptures, where it is clear the angels eat food. It was in Psalms and is clear that we are meat eaters, not them. I thought about their sleep habits. It seems as if they don't sleep. I worried about this because I love the feeling of sleep. But rest is the ultimate outcome, so what if we didn't sleep? Isn't the mystery the same thing? I mean, after all, you are "ENTERING INTO MY REST" and you don't think! wow! Mystery? I hadn't been doing it much the last few years. The fame had taken up a lot of my time. I needed to do it tonight. I needed to see the future. I needed to see what was going to happen tomorrow when mankind's mental telepathy chips were activated.

I got a little taste of the chaos already. Little Jimmy heard about a world-wide live broadcast on TV. They were looking for me. The world couldn't deal with the presence of all the flying saucers in the skies. They wanted me to come forward. I knew that I couldn't yet. I had to give them one night to think about the future. Unfortunately, religious chaos was happening everywhere. The Jehovah's Witnesses were right in the forefront with the demon movement. Little Jake turned on the television. There was one of them giving an interview. There were also people panicking in the background, screaming out "What will we do? What about tomorrow? What about our jobs? Do we go to work?" they screamed. "Do we go on with our normal lives and how can we live with this?" the bystander screamed as she looked up. The cameraman panned the sky. It was full of flying saucers.

The JW said not to worry, just get the Bible out and read, then pray to Jehovah. The reporter quickly said that I already had already written about this in my book and didn't buy it; he didn't buy it either. The JW said "JEHOVAH" would not let "HIS PEOPLE" down.

"Well, let's see," the reporter replied immediately. He got out a Bible and gave it to him. The JW didn't know what to do. The reporter did. He taunted him to take it. The guy couldn't move. His "BLIND FAITH" was really working. He obviously couldn't "SEE" it.

Anyway, he didn't take it. So, the reporter did it and nothing happened. The JW didn't give him a chance to ask anymore, and he left. The reporter turned to the camera and made an appeal directly to me. He had his cell phone ready. He wanted me to call. Little Jake immediately started sayin' "Call him, Daddy, call him!" He was so excited. I picked up the phone. Angel just looked at me. I knew that look, and it was all about interrupting dinner. I had to laugh deep down inside.

"Look who's coming to dinner tomorrow," I said to myself. I dialed the phone as she got up. Her mother did too. No, suddenly they both stopped. Thank God, uh the aliens, rather. They read my mind. I don't judge them; I love them! I'm ad-Dicted too! Brenda has helped us so much. Thanks, Brenda. I was about to tell the world that we would all read each other's minds tomorrow. I set up the event for tomorrow morning at nine a.m. I forewarned the world. We would also be able to see our past. Memory is science.

I did it. I did what I had to do. I revealed the truth about our species and ourselves. The world hated it. The night ended. I did mystery all night with my two boys, Mom, and Nurse Gail. Brian called. I couldn't let anyone find me. I needed to do mystery. I must know the mystery to the Kingdom of Heaven in order to teach it!

The next morning came and little Jake got his ride in the saucer. I made my appearance on the White House roof. I made my presentation, like a history teacher revealing the evidence of our past. I showed them our current technologies, like teleportation, cloaking devices, human creation, and finally BRAIN TRANSPLANTATION! I showed it all, but nothing could prepare them for the activation of the mental telepathy chip. I forewarned them that our sexual nature will wreak havoc only temporarily. It will be shut off quickly. But we will "SEE" why we are scientifically flawed as a result of it. The majority of the world will become violent as a result of immediate jealousy.

The chip was activated. All hell ensued, and the world saw it with their own eyes and "MIND"! It was done. I turned it off. I addressed the world again. Please don't resist our efforts to establish peace. Your way of life now is not dependent upon money, just your service to this transition. The tenth planet will cause a temporary reprieve for your current global warming. The Earth will remain a paradise for a little while longer. However, don't be fooled into thinking this Earth is permanent. Learn about the universe you live in. We need your help. Knowledge is power, but love is the most powerful thing of all. It is the emotion that will give you the ability to make this sacrifice. Knowledge is what will give you the strength. Please don't stop learning. Seek first the Kingdom of Heaven. We like the universe/

heaven are infinite. It's all mind over matter.

I LOVE YOU ALL!

Please look forward to my next book: "MICHAEL'S WAR IN HEAVEN" and my new video for those who don't like to read: PROOF: WHY THEY DON'T SHOW! I want to highly recommend Erich Von Daniken's *GOLD OF THE GODS*! It makes gold's importance to heaven very clear. I hope he doesn't get angry that I used his evidence without asking. He wants to know what these ancient astronauts look like. I think the evidence is very clear. In fact, it "SPEAKS FOR ITSELF."

Oh, by the way, if you want to know how to get to heaven, you're already there, since it's everywhere. But if you want to be with the father/fathers where there is no violence/death, then Yeshua made it very clear. He said this to the "JEWISH PREACHERS" who said they followed the Ten Commandments. He said, "There is then only one last thing to do, make yourself perfect and give away all that you have. Hardly shall a rich man enter the kingdom of heaven. Woe to the rich and blessed are the poor."

I'm sorry, this is just a scientific fact. Religion

is anti-man and anti-wealth! My research is finally dedicated to those who have lost loved ones in a freak tragic accident. I have two in my family and can hardly finish this without my body heaving in pain. I am crying as I type.

We all miss you so much Nancy Gail and Dan the Man! Peace, love and harmony to all!

Sincerely, Michael

P.S. Please look for my first film/documentary to be released July 4 in the summer of 2006 at the Roswell, New Mexico, film festival. It is titled "WHY THE BLANK DOESN'T ANYONE CARE?"

To purchase our latest DVD, contact Jeff Willes at 623-847-9132, my partner and film maker, one of the most honest and humble men I know. You're a great friend Jeff. Thanks,
Michael Brumfield
931-657-5815 or 931-261-6697

Proof

History teacher mike brumfield tells
his opinion of why the extraterrestrials
wont make open contact with the human
race
Also featuring the amazing ufo video footage
of jeff willes recorded over the phoenix az
area

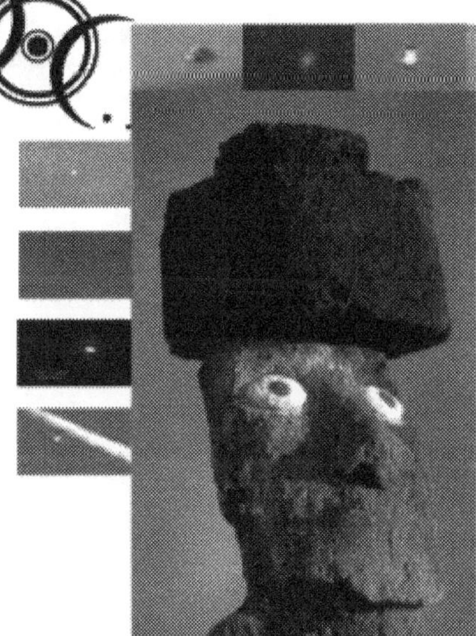

Sample Opinion:

World's largest ancient flying saucer:

Purpose: Tell us where they are up, just like Yeshua second coming on the clouds!

Look for upcoming DVD, *"Why The Blank Don't They Care."*

Truth is stranger than fiction.

See *Twilight Zone* episode, "Human Aliens with Big Eyes."

Art does indeed imitate life.
We are their artwork, and our art shows
us what they look like. See Easter Island heads
and their eyes match Twilight Zone episode, fifty years ago.

What they look like is
the ultimate question.
Art/science will have
the last word, even if
it tortures us all.

WWYD?